"Jessica, yesterday I thought I was going to a store to make sure my brother was okay. Since then, what was thought to be a robbery has snowballed into something that appears to be much deeper. I have to find out what's going on."

"How are you going to do that?" she asked.

He thought for a moment before he responded. "I think I'll take a few days' leave and poke around on my own. See what I can turn up."

She pushed out of her chair. "Well, I wish you luck. Let me know if I can help in any way."

He stood and faced her. "You can. How about working with me for a few days?"

She stared at him as if he'd lost his mind. "You can't be serious."

"I am. After all, Lee Tucker is a fugitive and you're a bounty hunter."

She stared into his eyes without blinking. "Ryan, I don't know..."

He reached for her hand and clasped it in his. "Please, Jessica. It'll be like old times. The two of us working on a case. What do you say? Want to be my partner again?"

Sandra Robbins is an award-winning, multipublished author of Christian fiction who lives with her husband in Tennessee. Without the support of her wonderful husband, four children and five grandchildren it would be impossible for her to write. It is her prayer that God will use her words to plant seeds of hope in the lives of her readers so they may come to know the peace she draws from her life.

Books by Sandra Robbins

Love Inspired Suspense

Bounty Hunters

Fugitive Trackdown
Fugitive at Large

Final Warning
Mountain Peril
Yuletide Defender
Dangerous Reunion
Shattered Identity
Fatal Disclosure

The Cold Case Files

Dangerous Waters
Yuletide Jeopardy
Trail of Secrets

Visit the Author Profile page at Harlequin.com.

FUGITIVE AT LARGE

SANDRA ROBBINS

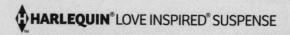
HARLEQUIN® LOVE INSPIRED® SUSPENSE

Recycling programs
for this product may
not exist in your area.

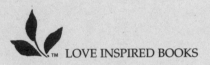

™ LOVE INSPIRED BOOKS

ISBN-13: 978-0-373-44687-2

Fugitive at Large

www.Harlequin.com

Printed in U.S.A.

Two are better than one; because they have a good reward for their labour. For if they fall, the one will lift up his fellow: but woe to him that is alone when he falleth; for he hath not another to help him up.

–Ecclesiastes 4:9-10

To Fran for all her encouragement

ONE

Being caught in a convenience-store robbery wasn't what Jessica Knight had expected when she stopped to get a soft drink. But from the panicked voices at the front of the store she thought that was exactly what was happening.

"What do you think you're doing, man?" Fear and disbelief combined in the shrill voice that drifted toward her from the direction of the checkout counter.

"I said give me the money in the cash register."

"Please, mister, just take it easy with that gun before somebody gets hurt." Jessica recognized the frightened voice of the young man who'd waited on her the past few times she'd stopped at the store.

"I'll take it easy when I have the money. Now put all the money in that bag," the robber snarled.

As of yet, the thief had no idea she was in the store, but that was about to change. She carefully closed the open door of the soft-drink display case and unzipped her heavy jacket. Her fingers curled around the gun holstered at her waist as she pulled it free.

Her mind whirled in indecision. What was her greatest chance of stopping the robbery in progress without anyone getting hurt? Shoot first and hope for the best, or try to talk the guy into surrendering his weapon? Whatever she decided, she had to act before somebody got shot or, worse, killed. It was time to make a move.

So much for staying hidden at the end of the aisle. She took a tentative step toward the front of the store. She knew the layout as well as she did that of her own apartment. The potato-chip display at the end of the aisle wasn't going to offer much protection from a bullet once she stepped into view. Better to surprise the thief before he had the chance to take a shot at her.

She gripped the gun with both hands and tiptoed farther forward, conscious of being absolutely silent. At the end of the aisle, she took a deep breath and peered toward the cash register about fifteen feet away. Behind the counter the pale clerk kept his eyes on the robber as he pulled bills from the cash register and stuffed them in a bag he held. The robber kept the gun trained on the young man as he reached up and pulled the ball cap he wore lower on his forehead.

A customer, possibly a college student from the campus nearby, stood in front of the counter with his hands raised. His fingers trembled. Scared out of his wits, no doubt. The hammering of her heart told her he wasn't the only one frightened.

The clerk swallowed hard and pushed the bag across the counter toward the gunman. "That's it unless you want the coins, too."

The robber shook his head. "No. That'll do just fine." He raised the gun and pointed it toward the clerk, who raised his hands and backed away.

"Leave him alone," the young customer said. "He did what you asked him to do."

The thief smiled. "Yes, he did."

He stared at the clerk for a moment before he reached for the bag. The moment his fingers touched the bag, the clerk took a step back and dropped to the floor behind the counter. Clutching the bag of money, the gunman whirled to face the customer and pointed the gun at him.

The young man lowered his hands and put them out in front of him as if to shield his body from the gun's blast. "No. Please, no." His whispered plea sent chills through Jessica.

The robber smiled and shook his head. "You shouldn't have stuck your nose in where it doesn't belong."

He raised the gun and pointed it toward the young man's head.

Jessica's hope that she could do something to keep anyone from being hurt evaporated. The intent of the robber was plain. He meant to kill the young man standing at the counter and possibly the clerk also.

She took a deep breath and stepped out into the open. "Drop your gun, or I'll shoot!" she yelled.

A surprised look flashed on the robber's face, and he jerked the gun away from the customer and aimed it at her. Before she could move, the sharp crack of a bullet exploded next to her, and the smell of barbe-cued potato chips filled the air. She ducked and fired at the gunman before he had the chance to get off a better-aimed shot.

A scream of pain poured from the robber's mouth. He dropped the gun and the bag of money before he grabbed for the side of his head. Jessica could see a

trail of blood running down the man's cheek and realized her bullet must have grazed his head.

She took a step forward, and the man stooped to re-
trieve his gun. She raised hers higher and stared down
the barrel of the weapon. "Don't even think about it,
mister."

He cast a wild-eyed stare from her to the customer.
Then he grabbed the young man and shoved him toward her. She braced for the impact, but the boy's full
weight slammed into her and knocked her backward.

The robber, blood still trickling from his head, turned
and ran out the door before she could regain her footing.
Jessica caught a glimpse of the young customer's fear-
filled eyes before she darted around him and sprinted
after the fleeing gunman.

The clerk peeked up over the top of the counter as
she sped past. "Call 911," she yelled over her shoulder.

As she stepped onto the sidewalk outside the store,
she saw the thief run toward the open passenger door
of a waiting car. He jumped into the car, and it peeled
away before he had the door closed. She lowered her
gun and stared at the car's license plate. As she muttered the numbers on the plate over and over, she
pulled a notepad with an attached pen out of her pocket
and jotted them down in an unsteady hand.

When she walked back in the store, the clerk was
leaning against the counter, his face in his hands. The
bag containing the money lay on the floor where the
robber had dropped it when he fired the first shot.
The customer stood in front of the cash register, his
face pale and his body trembling. His hand clutched a
cell phone, and he glanced down at it. "I called 911."

Jessica glanced at the clerk, and he bit down on his

lip. "I was shaking so hard I couldn't get my fingers to work." He sagged against the now-closed cash register and shuddered. "Did he get away?" he mumbled.

"Yes. Someone was waiting outside in a car." She grasped the young customer's shoulder and gave it a squeeze. "Are you okay?"

He straightened to his full height and nodded. His gaze drifted to the gun still in her hand and then back to her face. His lips moved, but no sound emerged from his mouth. He cleared his throat and looked at the gun once more. "Who are you? A police officer?"

She stuck her gun back in the holster and shook her head. "Not anymore. I used to be. Now I'm a bounty hunter."

His eyes widened and his mouth gaped open. Jessica tried to suppress the smile that always accompanied the surprised first reaction of many people when she told them her profession. She knew what the next question would be, and he didn't disappoint her.

"A woman bounty hunter?"

She sighed in resignation. "Yes, believe it or not. There are women who take on this job, and I'm proud to say I'm one of them."

The clerk shook his head in disbelief. "I've been seeing you come in here for a while, but I never would have guessed you were a bounty hunter. Are you like that guy on TV? You know, the one who tracks down fugitives who've skipped bail."

She shrugged. "A bit like him. I don't have tattoos like he does, though."

The two young men smiled.

"Well, whatever you do for a living," the customer

said, "I'm glad you were here today. You saved our lives." He stuck out his hand. "My name's Jamie."

She grasped his hand and shook it. "And I'm Jessica."

The clerk gave a shaky laugh. "And I'm Richard."

He started to say something else, but before he could, sirens wailed outside and tires squealed as a car came to a stop. "Sounds like the police have arrived. That was fast," she said.

She stepped toward the entrance to meet the first responders and had almost reached it when the front door burst open. A man bolted inside, then skidded to an abrupt stop, the surprise on his face reflecting her own. Neither one of them spoke for a moment, and then he drew in a rough breath.

"Jessica?"

Her eyes wide, she took a step back and shook her head. This couldn't be happening. Ryan Spencer. Why hadn't she expected him to come? After all, the store was in the precinct where he worked. Where *she'd* worked when they'd been partners four years ago. Her fingers curled into her palms, and she swallowed.

She hadn't spoken to him in four years and hadn't seen him in nearly a year. The last time she'd laid eyes on him had been when a man broke into her apartment determined to kill her best friend, Claire Walker, who happened to be staying with her at the time. Ryan had answered the call. They hadn't talked that night. And now here he was again. Not changed a bit, and still as handsome as ever.

His dark hair fell across his forehead just as she remembered. And as she knew he would, he reached up and raked it back as he did every time he was nervous. His gaze drifted over her again. He started to speak, but she beat him to it.

She cleared her throat, lifted her chin and stepped forward. "Hello, Ryan. Since when does a detective arrive at a crime scene first?"

He glanced at the young man next to the checkout counter. "I was only a block away."

"So you thought you'd beat everybody else to the scene." Her lips curled into a sneer. "Why does that not surprise me?" She glanced over her shoulder at the clerk and customer who still stood at the checkout counter, then returned her gaze to the detective. "Then don't let me detain you. I'll go see about that soft drink I was about to purchase when all the excitement started."

She turned to leave, but he reached out and touched her arm. "Wait, Jessica. I wanted to thank you."

She turned around and frowned down at his hand on her arm. "Thank me? For what?"

He released his hold on her. "The dispatcher said a woman in the store prevented the robber from shooting a customer. I wanted to meet that woman and thank her."

Something in the way he said the words made her uneasy, and she narrowed her eyes. "It was nothing, really. I'm glad I was here to prevent it from happening."

He shook his head. "You're wrong. It wasn't nothing. Not to me anyway."

"I don't understand," she said.

He pointed toward the young customer. "That college kid you just kept from being murdered is Jamie Spencer. He's my brother."

Ryan felt a quick stab of disappointment. Jessica's startled look told him she'd had no idea Jamie was his brother.

Her eyebrows arched, and she glanced toward his brother, who had a big smile on his face. "Th-that's *your* Jamie?"

He nodded. "Yeah. I guess you never got to meet him when we were working together."

The surprise he'd seen on her face moments ago vanished at his reference to their former relationship. "Working together?" she muttered. "I guess you could call it that."

He started to say something else, but Jamie called out to him. "Ryan, how did you know about this?"

Ryan glanced past her and smiled at his brother. "Sally Douglas took the 911 call, and she notified me. I was only a block away."

He glanced back at Jessica, and a slight smile pulled at her lips. "Sally's still taking care of everybody, huh?" she asked.

He nodded. "Yes, and she likes Jamie. I guess I'd forgotten that you never did meet my brother. He was fifteen when he came to live with me."

She darted a glance at Jamie and then back to him. "Of course I knew about him, but I never saw him. At the time, you said he was going through a rebellious phase, and you thought I might want to wait to meet him. And then we…" She hesitated. "We…"

"We ended our partnership," he finished for her.

Her eyes clouded, and she pursed her lips in a look

of distaste. "Not we. You." The words hit him like barbs. "You were the one who ended it."

She still couldn't see the truth. Or maybe she'd never wanted to see the truth. At any rate, what difference did it make now? He took a deep breath.

"I guess we still have differing opinions on that," he said. "But that happened four years ago. We've both come out of that bad time no worse for wear. At least you look like you have." He glanced over her, then back at Jamie. "At any rate, I still want to thank you for saving my brother's life. I'm sure he's very appreciative, too."

She waved her hand in dismissal. "I'm just glad he wasn't hurt. Now, why don't you go tell him how glad you are he's okay. I'll wait for the officers to arrive and give them my statement. I'm sure they'll let me know if I'm needed later on."

She whirled around and strode to the back of the store. The potato chips that covered the floor crunched under her feet as she disappeared down one of the aisles. He stared after her for a moment, and then he sighed and turned toward his brother.

Jamie straightened from leaning against the cash register as he approached, and Ryan enveloped him in a big bear hug. "Are you okay?"

Jessica reappeared, a soft drink in her hand, and walked past them toward the front door. She didn't glance at them as she passed, but Ryan couldn't tear his eyes off her.

Jamie drew his attention when he spoke. "Yeah, I'm fine. Thanks to Jessica. I saw you talking to her. Did you thank her for helping me today?"

"I did. You're lucky to be alive. These convenience-store robberies don't always end this well."

Jamie grinned and glanced in the direction Jessica had gone. "It might go better if there were more customers like her in the stores. Did you know she's a bounty hunter?"

Ryan nodded. "Yeah. She was a police officer before that."

"I know. She told us. Did you know her then, Ryan?"

He hesitated before he answered. He'd thought he'd known her then. But could anyone say with certainty they knew another person? He thought she would understand why he did what he did, but he'd been wrong.

Ryan debated the question for a moment before he responded. "She was my partner."

A shocked look washed across Jamie's face. "Your partner? You never said anything to me about having a woman partner."

Ryan shrugged. "It was a long time ago. You were a teenager and had other things on your mind instead of who my partner at the time happened to be."

At that moment the front door opened, and two Memphis PD officers stepped inside. He watched as they stopped next to Jessica. "I want to hear what Jessica has to say to the officers. I'll be back in a minute."

He walked over to her and nodded at Officer Jimmy Austin, who stood facing her. "Hi, Jimmy. I thought I'd listen to Jessica's statement if that's okay."

The officer nodded. "Sure, Ryan. Sally said your brother was here when the robbery occurred. Is that right?"

"Yeah, he's standing over there by the cash register."

"Then I'll get his statement after I talk to Jessica." He turned to his partner and nodded toward her. "This is Jessica Knight," he explained. "She used to work out of our precinct. One of the best detectives I've ever seen. She—" He stopped himself and his mouth formed a small O as a thought must have hit him. He wagged his finger first at Ryan and then Jessica. "Didn't the two of you used to be partners?"

Jessica stiffened. "Yes, but that was a long time ago."

The air seemed to have taken on a frost, but Jimmy's face flushed. "Oh, right." He cleared his throat and took a deep breath. "Well, let's get this over with. Are there any other witnesses besides you and Ryan's brother?" he asked Jessica.

She pointed to the clerk. "Richard. He works here. Just the three of us."

Jimmy glanced at his partner and jerked his head in Jamie and the clerk's direction. "Why don't you get their statements. I'll take Jessica's."

The other officer nodded and looked at Jessica. "Nice to meet you, ma'am. I've heard a lot about you. The guys said you're working with your brothers over at the Knight Agency now. Is that right?"

"It is. I decided I'd let you guys catch the criminals, and I'll go after them if they skip bail."

Jimmy laughed. "Don't be fooled by this lady. She's tough as nails, just like her two brothers. In fact, her twin brother, Lucas, is a friend of mine. We ride motorcycles together a lot. I don't know how many times he's told me about the bounty-hunter business his great-grandfather started and the slogan he lived by."

Jessica smiled. "'A man must answer for the crimes laid against him,'" she said. "We still believe that."

Ryan wondered how many times during the years he and Jessica worked together he had heard her say those words. "So do we cops," he said.

She jerked her head around and glared at him before she turned back to Jimmy. "Okay, let's get this over with. I remember the drill. So let me tell you what happened."

For the next few minutes she gave her account of what had happened as well as a detailed description of the robber. Ryan concentrated on the details and watched as Jimmy took notes from time to time. When she finished, Ryan spoke up. "And you got the car license number?"

"I did." She pulled her notepad from her pocket and read off the numbers to him.

Jimmy looked up from the notes he'd been writing. "Could you come down to the station tomorrow and look at some mug shots to see if you recognize the holdup guy?"

"Sure," Jessica said. "Whatever you need me to do."

"Come to my office," Ryan said. "I'll have them ready for you."

Jimmy glanced at his notes again. "And you say the robber was wounded?"

"Yes, but it wasn't bad. I think the bullet grazed his head."

"We'll notify the hospitals to be on the lookout for a gunshot wound to the side of the head."

Jessica shrugged. "I suppose you should, but I doubt if he'll go to a hospital. He can probably treat it with first aid. I might have gotten a better shot at him if I hadn't had all those potato chips flying in my face."

"Potato chips." Ryan laughed and looked back at the chips that now lay in scattered crumbs across the floor. "You always did have a sense of humor. But seriously, I'm glad you were here today. My brother probably wouldn't be alive if you hadn't stepped forward."

"Just doing what I've been trained to do."

Her words had a jagged edge to them, and he wondered if she was trying to deliver an unspoken message to him. Did she resent him because she thought she would still be in police work if it hadn't been for him?

"I'm sure you remember how upsetting it was to enter a robbery scene and find victims who'd been shot for no other reason than for being in the wrong place at the wrong time," he told her. "No one was shot today. And that was because of you. Thank you, Jessica."

She didn't say anything for a moment. Then she touched Jimmy's arm as he took a step toward the witnesses. "Jimmy, I was wondering. I've had a busy day, and I'm tired. You have my statement about what happened and my description of the robber. Would it be okay if I go on home? If you need anything else, you know where to find me."

Jimmy thought a moment before he nodded. "Sure, Jessica. Go on. We'll be in touch if we need anything else. I'm always glad to see that no one was hurt in a robbery. We have you to thank for that."

"Thanks. I think I'll go say goodbye to Jamie and Richard before I leave."

Ryan moved out of her way as she stepped around him and headed over to where Jamie stood. He smiled when she stopped next to him. "I'm going home, but I wanted to say goodbye first."

Jamie reached out and grabbed her hand. "Thank you for everything, Jessica. You were great."

She waved her hand in dismissal. "It was nothing. I'm glad the two of you are okay. Take care of yourselves and remember to be mindful of your surroundings no matter where you are."

Jamie smiled and nodded. "I will."

She glanced at Richard. "I need to pay for my drink."

He shook his head and laughed. "It's on the house. You've earned it."

She raised the bottle in a salute to him. "Thanks."

Jamie stopped her as she turned to leave. "Wait a minute, Jessica. I wanted to ask you something. My brother told me you used to be his partner. Do you ever miss being on the force?" Her face flushed, and Jamie gave a little gasp. "I'm sorry. I didn't mean to be so nosy. It's just that you handled yourself so well today, I think you must have been a good police officer."

Before she could respond, Ryan spoke up from behind her. "She was good. The best partner I ever had. I hated to see her leave police work."

Jessica stared at him a moment as he came to stand beside her. Then she turned back to Jamie. "I like what I do now. It's rewarding work, and I get to work with people I love and admire."

A teasing glint sparkled in Jamie's eyes. "And you still get to carry a gun."

Jessica laughed. "And I still get to carry a gun. I'm so used to it that it's become a part of me. In fact, I carry it with me all the time."

"Lucky for all of us," Jamie said. "It was nice meeting you, Jessica."

"Nice meeting you, too, Jamie."

Then she turned and walked toward the door, her words about working with people whom she loved and admired still ringing in Ryan's ears. Her meaning hadn't been lost on him. She hadn't loved him or even held him in very high regard. He pressed his lips together and didn't say anything as he watched her go.

When she'd disappeared out the door, he turned back to his brother, who was staring at him with a slight smile curling his lips.

"I don't know what happened between you two," Jamie said, "but it must have been bad. There was enough heat in her voice to singe the hairs on my arms. What did you do to her anyway?"

"Nothing," Ryan muttered.

"Nothing? I know women can be hard to understand at times, but I didn't have any trouble getting her message. She doesn't like you at all. You must have done something to make her feel that way."

Ryan reached over and pounded his fist against the countertop. The officers talking to the clerk whirled at the sound and stared at him.

"Spencer, are you okay?" one of the men asked.

He rubbed his hand across his eyes. "I'm fine.

Still a little rattled over how close my brother came to dying."

They nodded and went back to their questioning.

Jamie stared at Ryan and frowned. "I'm sorry if I said the wrong thing. I just thought Jessica seemed like such a nice person."

"She is a nice person. We had a disagreement, and it's never been solved."

Jamie narrowed his eyes. "Oh, I see. Then maybe it's time you did something about that. From the way she reacted to that robber and took control of the entire situation, I'd say there aren't many women around like her."

"You're right about that. There aren't many like her."

Jamie stepped closer and lowered his voice. "Do you remember when I first came to live with you after Mom and Dad were killed and I had so many problems adjusting?"

Ryan chuckled. "How could I forget? You nearly drove me crazy for two years."

"Yeah, I gave you a lot of trouble. But you didn't give up on me. And when I'd come home telling you about how everybody was against me, you always made me face up to my own mistakes. You didn't make excuses for me and wouldn't let me make them for myself. Maybe it's time you quit making excuses for whatever you did to Jessica and try to make it right."

Ryan shook his head. "I don't know if I can or not."

Jamie punched him on the shoulder and grinned. "You'll never know unless you try. What have you got to lose? The worst thing that can happen is that she'll hate you more than she already does."

Ryan stared at his brother in surprise. "When did you get so smart?"

Jamie laughed and shrugged. "I always have been. I just didn't want you to know it. Now, do as I say and get things straightened out with Jessica."

He thought for a moment about what his brother had said, then turned to him and smiled. "Maybe I will. Maybe I will."

Turning away from Jamie, he walked to the front door and stared out at Jessica as she climbed into her car, which was parked to the left of the entrance. She sat behind the steering wheel for a moment as if deep in thought before she finally started the ignition and backed out of her parking space.

As he watched her car disappear down the street, he thought of how he'd wrestled for the past four years with the decision of whether or not to try one more time to mend his relationship with Jessica. She'd been the best friend he'd ever had, and he missed her. But there was no getting around the fact that she didn't miss him.

Did he dare try again to explain his side of their misunderstanding?

After a moment, he inhaled and muttered to himself, "It's time to set the past straight. And this time, Jessica Knight, I'm not taking no for an answer. You are going to listen to me."

TWO

Jessica pulled into her parking space behind the apartment complex where she lived, turned off the ignition and stared at the walkway that led through what she supposed some people might call a backyard. Not her, though. To her a backyard was a wide-open lawn with flower beds in the spring and shade trees to sit underneath in the summer. But the crowning touch would be a child's swing set and a grill for barbecues.

She lay back against the headrest and closed her eyes as she let her imagination fly to the life she wanted to have one day. Right now, though, it seemed as if her dreams would never come true. She was twenty-eight years old, almost twenty-nine, and she hadn't had a serious boyfriend since high school. The guy she'd dated in college didn't count because he didn't like her brothers, and that was a deal breaker for her.

Her parents had worried when she became a police officer. Even more so when she joined the Knight Agency as a bounty hunter. They feared what might happen to her. And it almost had today. That bullet had come way too close.

Her hands tightened on the steering wheel as she

recalled the rush of air across her face and the smell of barbecued potato chips when the bullet struck the rack beside her. Her body began to shake as the scene in the store replayed in her mind. Why was she suddenly reacting this way?

Post-traumatic shock, she told herself. That was what it was. She'd studied it when she was a police officer and knew it was likely to happen after suffering an event where a person felt intense fear or horror. She also knew that it occurred more in women than in men.

But was that really what was wrong with her? She'd faced dangerous situations before and had never had this feeling of powerlessness. Maybe she was just tired and needed some rest.

Or maybe it was something else. Something she didn't want to recognize.

Shaking her head in denial, she stepped from the car and headed down the short flagstone walkway that led toward the back door of her apartment. As she stepped onto the porch, she looked over her shoulder at the small grassy area the complex owners advertised as a yard. It wasn't what she envisioned as a garden area, but it was okay for now. Maybe it was time to start looking for a new place with a backyard big enough for her to putter around in when she wasn't working.

With a sigh she slipped the key in the lock and was about to walk through the back door when she heard the sound of a car engine. She glanced over her shoulder and stared at the black SUV that drove slowly past the parked cars behind the complex. It stopped when it reached near where her car was parked and sat there, its engine idling.

Jessica squinted to get a better look inside, but she couldn't see past the tinted windows. The hair at the back of her neck stood up. Had someone followed her home?

She unzipped her jacket and pushed it back to expose the gun at her waist. The only reaction she received was the revving of the engine, but the car remained still. Frowning, Jessica stepped down from the back porch onto the brick walkway. The engine rumbled again, but the car still didn't move.

Jessica's heart pounded as she took one more step, then another. She was just about to pull her gun from its holster when the window on the passenger side slid down. A young woman stuck her head out through the opening and called out, "Excuse me, ma'am. Could you tell me where apartment 4-G is?"

Stunned, Jessica came to an abrupt halt and stared at the girl. The Greek letters on the front of her sweatshirt were the same as Jessica had seen on other girls walking across the nearby college campus.

"4-G?" she asked as she inched closer.

The girl smiled, and Jessica could see another girl in the driver's seat. Her sweatshirt was identical to her friend's. "Yes, one of our sorority sisters is moving in there, and we said we'd help out. But we haven't been able to find it yet."

Jessica released the hold she had on her weapon and pointed down the street. "Go around the end of this building and then turn to the left. It should be on the far end."

The girl glanced over her shoulder at her friend and

laughed. "I told you to go that way, but you wouldn't listen." She turned back to Jessica. "Thank you, ma'am."

Jessica gave a weak wave and tried to smile. "No problem."

She stood still and stared after the car as it moved off in the direction she'd pointed. After a few minutes she shook her head and chuckled. What was the matter with her? Had the incident at the convenience store upset her so much that she'd mistaken a simple request for directions to have some sinister motive?

If she had been as observant as she should, she would have been following the advice she'd given Jamie Spencer earlier—be aware of your surroundings. Then she would have known she wasn't being followed.

Sighing, she touched her gun once more and headed toward the back door. If the convenience-store episode had taught her nothing else, it had reminded her to be more alert to what was happening around her.

She stopped on the small back porch and took a long look over her shoulder. Nothing there. Nobody following her. But she still had an uneasy feeling that something wasn't quite right. She stood there for a few minutes, the scenario from the convenience store playing over and over in her head.

Something wasn't right about the robbery. But what was it?

One of the first things she'd learned as a police officer was to trust her instincts when it came to solving a case. And right now some sixth sense was telling her she was overlooking something.

After a few minutes she shook her head. Whatever it was would come to her, probably at the least likely moment.

She unlocked the door and stepped inside. The house felt warm and inviting after the cool temperature outside. She took off her coat and hung it on the back of a kitchen chair and was about to take her gun off when the front doorbell rang.

Jessica pulled the gun from her holster and eased from the kitchen into the living room and over to the apartment's front door. The smell of barbecued potato chips enveloped her, and it was as if she was back in the store with a gun pointed at her. No way was she going to open the door without knowing who was on the other side.

Taking a deep breath and holding it, she stared through the peephole. The breath she'd been holding escaped her body in a big rush, and she sagged against the door. For the second time today she'd experienced a complete surprise.

Slowly she unlocked the door and pulled it open. "What are you doing here?" she asked.

Ryan stared back at her, and then his gaze dropped to the gun she still held. His forehead wrinkled, and he tilted his head to one side. "Do you always answer the door with a gun in your hand?"

"Of course not. I had just gotten home and was taking it off."

He nodded. "Oh, I see."

She straightened her back. "You haven't answered my question. What are you doing here?"

He swallowed, and his Adam's apple bobbed. "I want to talk to you, Jessica. May I come in?"

She started to refuse but then thought better of it.

She shrugged, opened the door wider and stepped aside for him to enter. "I guess so."

He stepped into the apartment and waited until she'd closed the door. Without speaking, he followed her into the living room, where she gave a jerk of her head, indicating for him to sit on the sofa. She took a chair facing him.

His gaze drifted over the apartment, and he smiled. "You have a nice place here. I don't know if you re-member or not, but I was here about a year ago."

"I remember."

"Your friend Claire Walker was almost killed that night trying to bring in a bail jumper on her own, and your brother Adam saved her life. He brought her here so she'd be safe, but the fugitive found her. He broke in and tried to kill her. Thanks to you that didn't happen."

Jessica frowned and shook her head. "Claire and I have always made a great team. She helped fight him off, too."

He nodded. "Yeah, I remember that's what you said. How's she doing now?"

"Fine. She and my brother Adam are married, and she's working at the agency with us."

His eyes lit up, and he smiled. "That's great. I hope they'll be happy. I always liked Adam and Lucas. You're lucky to have such great brothers."

"You have a nice brother, too. I was surprised today to find out who he is. He's not anything like the teen-age kid you used to talk about after he first came to live with you."

Ryan chuckled and shook his head. "No, he's grown up a lot. Back then he was having a lot of problems dealing with all the changes in his life. You know,

Mom's and Dad's deaths and having to change schools when he came to live with me. But I'm proud of the way he's turned out. He's in college and works on the school newspaper. He also has a part-time job working at a computer store."

"I'm glad things have improved for the two of you. But is that what you came to tell me?"

His face flushed, and he glanced down at his hands. "No. I came because Jamie told me I needed to."

Jessica frowned and settled back farther in her chair in hopes of displaying an attitude of indifference. Her nonchalance seemed to be working. She spotted a small trickle of perspiration roll down the side of Ryan's face, and she almost laughed.

"Why would he tell you that?" Jessica asked.

"Because he thought you were so brave to take on that robber and you were kind to him afterward. Then he saw how you changed when I arrived. He wanted to know what that was all about."

"What did you tell him?"

"That we had a misunderstanding a few years ago, and you've held me responsible ever since. When he asked if I'd tried to fix things between us, I told him I hadn't. He said it was time I quit making excuses and made things right. I've known for a long time I should do that, but I haven't, and I'm sorry about that. Once, we shared something special, and I know I was the one who ruined it. I've faced the fact that we can never go back to where we were, but I would like for us to be friends, Jessica. It's time we talked through whatever happened between us and made peace with each other."

She studied his face. He looked sincere. But could

she be sure? Once, she had loved him. Not only had she trusted him with her heart, but as her partner, she'd trusted him with her life. That was a long time ago, and a lot had happened since then. She didn't know if there was any way they could ever be friends, and certainly they could never go back to the closeness they'd once shared.

After a moment, she pushed to her feet and shook her head. "I don't think there's any reason we need to continue this conversation. Let's just say that we didn't know each other as well as we thought we did and leave it at that. Now, I think you'd better leave."

She turned to lead him to the door, but he sprang from the sofa and grabbed her by the arm. When she faced him, she almost gasped aloud at the anguish she saw in his eyes.

"No," he said. "This isn't going to end like the other times when I tried to make you understand. You're going to let me speak. Then I'll leave and never bother you again. But this once, will you put that stubborn Knight pride away and listen to what I have to say?"

Jessica didn't move for a moment as her gaze drifted over his face. His eyes seemed to be pleading with her to remember the good times they'd had together, the laughter they'd shared and the feeling that maybe they'd stumbled upon something they'd both been searching for.

Then his parents were killed, and his attitude toward her changed. The pain she'd tried to ignore for the past four years stabbed at her heart as she remembered the cold tone of his voice as he told her they needed to put their personal relationship on hold while he dealt with the loss. Even though she was devastated, she'd tried to understand what he was going through. At least, she told herself, they'd still be working together, and she could help him work through his grief.

It didn't take her long to realize he wasn't about to let that happen. He'd wanted her out of his life on all levels, and it had broken her heart. Now he said he wanted to make things right. It was too late for that, but perhaps not too late to understand why it had all ended.

She pulled her arm free of his grasp and sat down in her chair. She leaned back, crossed her legs and folded her hands in her lap. "Okay, Ryan, I'll listen. Maybe it's time I understood why you asked to have me taken off the Harvey murder case we were investigating."

He couldn't believe how cold her eyes looked when she spit the accusation at him. He raked his hand through his hair and sat down on the sofa facing her. He scooted to the edge of the cushion and rested his arms on his knees.

"The first thing you need to know is that I never asked for you to be removed from the case."

"Then why—"

He held up his hand for her to be silent. "Never. Let me say it again. I *never* asked to have you removed. I asked to be moved to another case and let you continue to work on finding Cal and Susan Harvey's killer. The captain made the choice to move you to another partner and let me stay where I was."

"That's not the way it was told to me. The captain said you thought it was better if we didn't work together anymore. When he told me that, I knew if you felt that way about me I couldn't stay at the precinct and see you every day."

"So you asked for a transfer."

"I did. I thought maybe you'd stop me before it was granted, but you didn't."

"I wanted to explain."

She sat up straight and stared at him. "Then why didn't you?"

A scoffing laugh rumbled in his throat. "When I heard you were leaving the precinct, I came to you, but you wouldn't listen. I don't remember how many times I tried. The last time I made the effort to tell you, I came to your apartment, but you told me to never come near you again and slammed the door in my face."

Her cheeks turned crimson, and she smiled sheepishly. "I remember. I think I also told you I'd have my brothers beat you up."

"Yeah, but I knew they wouldn't, even if you told them to."

"But why did you ask to be removed from the case?"

Even after all these years he still found it hard to talk about his emotional state at that time in his life. "Do you remember what had happened right before we took on the Harvey case?"

"Yes," she murmured. "Your parents were killed in a car wreck, and you had to take custody of your brother."

He nodded. "Jamie, the one you met today. It was a terrible time for me. My folks were dead, and my teenage brother was beside himself not only with grief but over having to move to another neighborhood and change schools."

"Why didn't you move into your parents' home so he didn't have so many changes in his life? Wouldn't that have been easier?"

"I thought about it. Unfortunately, the neighborhood had gone down a lot, and Jamie had started hanging out with a rough crowd. It was only a matter of time until he got into trouble. Dad had bought a new house out east of town right before he and Mom were killed in that wreck. He wanted to give Jamie a new start in another school. When I found myself as Jamie's guardian, I thought we could live in my apartment since it was in a better neighborhood, but Jamie was unhappy there. He did everything he could to defy me. I couldn't figure out how to make him understand I loved him and only wanted to help him. Out of desperation we finally moved to the house that Dad had bought. It turned out to be the best thing for Jamie. He made new friends and settled down."

"Why didn't you tell me all this?"

He shrugged. "Because it was my problem, not yours."

"But, Ryan," Jessica said, "I would have helped you."

Ryan shook his head. "I didn't want that. I was scared to death. Scared I couldn't get Jamie straightened out. And scared I couldn't be the kind of man you deserved in your life."

"What do you mean by that?"

"You have a great family, Jessica. Your brothers aren't afraid to tackle anything, and you're just like them. I knew you had high expectations for the guy you would marry, and my mind was in such turmoil that I knew I couldn't give you what you needed."

"Ryan, you were wrong."

He paused and closed his eyes for a moment, then took a deep breath. "Maybe so, but I wasn't thinking straight, and I found myself making mistakes on the job. And I couldn't forget how my last partner had died."

Jessica leaned forward and stared at Ryan. "You're still blaming yourself for Al Stevenson's death? It wasn't your fault that he was killed."

Ryan pushed to his feet and gritted his teeth. "He was my partner. If I'd been covering him like I should have, that drug dealer never would have gotten the drop on him."

Jessica rose to her feet and shook her head. "You're wrong, Ryan. I read the reports. Nobody blamed you for what happened. If he had waited for backup instead of leaving you to guard the front of the building and going in alone after a crazy killer, he might be alive today."

"I blamed myself," he said. "I still do."

"But that's ridiculous."

Ryan's hands were shaking, and he shoved them in his pockets. "It's not ridiculous. At the time, I was an emotional mess. I was still dealing with my guilt about Al's death when my parents died and I found myself the sole guardian of a troubled teenager. I began to question whether or not I should even stay in police work. But most of all, I didn't want you to get hurt."

Her eyes grew wide. "I don't understand."

"I didn't want you ending up like Al. Dead because I'd made another mistake. I couldn't have lived with that."

Jessica looked at him intently. She clasped her hands and squeezed until her knuckles turned white. Finally she spoke. "Oh, Ryan, I'm so sorry. I never knew how much you suffered because of Al's death. I wish I could have helped you with that. In time you'll come to see it wasn't your fault."

"I doubt if that time will ever come." After a moment, he took a deep breath. "That's all I wanted to tell you tonight. I didn't want to go another day with you thinking I'd stabbed you in the back to get you taken off the case we were working on. I didn't do it, Jessica. Please believe me. I've come to realize I missed out on the best thing I could have had in my life when I pushed you away. I know it's too late now to go back. But whatever I did at the time, I thought it was for your benefit. I hope in time you can come to forgive me."

"You've given me a lot to think about, but I still have questions."

"Maybe I can answer them. But I think that's enough soul baring for tonight. I need to get out of here and let you get some rest. It's been a hard day."

"Yes, it has. Perhaps we can get together sometime."

"That sounds like a brush-off to me." He exhaled a long breath and shook his head. "Listen, I won't bother you again, but I'd like to hear from you after you think about what I've said. Give me a call."

She opened her mouth to respond, but before she could, his cell phone rang. He pulled it from his pocket and stared at the caller ID. "Jamie's calling," he said. "I'd better take this."

He connected to the call and pressed the phone to his ear. "Hi, Jamie."

"Ryan, where are you?"

Jamie's words vibrated in his ear, and he frowned at what he thought sounded like anxiety. "I'm at Jessica's apartment. What's the matter?"

"I wanted to let you know I have to go out of town for a few days."

Ryan clutched the cell phone tighter. "Out of town? Where are you going?"

"I think it's better that you don't know. I'll call in a few days and let you know how I'm doing."

"Jamie," Ryan almost yelled into the phone. "What's going on? You can't leave town. You need to come down to headquarters in the morning and look at mug shots. Besides, you barely escaped being killed today. You need time to come to grips with what happened."

"Don't worry, Ryan. I'll be all right."

"Jamie!" Ryan yelled. "Jamie!"

But it was no use. His brother had disconnected the call. Still holding the phone, Ryan let his arm drift down to his side.

"Jamie's going out of town?" Jessica asked.

Ryan nodded. "That's what he said."

"But why?"

"I don't know. He wouldn't tell me. He said it was better if I didn't know."

He slipped the cell phone back in his pocket and turned to Jessica. "Thanks for seeing me. I think I'll—" He stopped midsentence when he saw the look on Jessica's face. Her eyes were wide and her face had turned as pale as a harvest moon. He reached out and grasped her arm. "What's the matter?"

A shiver ripped through her body, and she took a deep, shaky breath. "Call him back, Ryan," she said with urgency in her tone. "Tell him not to go. He needs to stay where you can keep an eye on him."

Her face had grown whiter, and a terrified look now gleamed in her eyes. He leaned closer to her. "Why?"

Her tongue licked at her lips, and in that moment he remembered how she always looked when she had suddenly unearthed a piece of evidence in a case.

"Ever since I left the store, something hasn't seemed right about what went down there. I've racked my brain trying to figure out what was bothering me, and now I understand what I was missing."

"Understand what, Jessica?"

"I didn't witness a robbery this afternoon. It was an attempted murder of your brother."

THREE

Jessica flinched at the shocked look on Ryan's face. He blinked at her and shook his head before he spoke. "What are you talking about? Why would anyone want to kill my brother?"

"I don't know, but now that I put everything together, it all makes sense."

He reached out and wrapped his fingers around her arms. "What things? Tell me."

She guided him back to the sofa and sat down beside him. "There were some little things about what went down at the store that I didn't understand. From where I was standing, I had a clear view of the robbery scene. The clerk put the money in the bag and laid it on the counter, but the robber didn't pick it up right away. Instead, he pointed the gun at the clerk, and Jamie told him to leave the guy alone, that he'd done what the man wanted. Then the gunman looked up at the clerk, Richard, and nodded. Richard dropped to the floor behind the counter like a ton of bricks, and the robber turned toward Jamie."

"What did he do next?"

"He kind of chuckled and aimed the gun at Jamie.

Then he said, 'You shouldn't have stuck your nose in where it doesn't belong.' I thought he meant interrupting him from shooting the clerk, but now I'm not so sure."

"You think the clerk was in on it?"

She thought for a moment before she answered. "Yes. I don't think the robber meant Jamie's interference in stopping him from shooting. I think it was something else. And whatever it happens to be, it was serious enough to get him killed."

Ryan shook his head. "This is pure speculation. Jamie is a college student. How could he get into trouble?"

"Do you know anything about his friends? Could he be in some kind of trouble?"

Ryan shook his head. "I don't think so. He doesn't go out much with friends. He spends most of his time working at the computer shop or writing articles for the school newspaper. I have no idea if he's mixed up in something or not."

"Then you must keep Jamie from going out of town," she said. "If somebody's watching him, they could kill him and dispose of his body somewhere. You wouldn't even know where to begin your search for him because he wouldn't tell you where he was going."

"You're right. I have to stop him." Ryan grabbed his cell phone and punched in Jamie's number. She heard it ring several times before it went to voice mail. Ryan grimaced and waited until the greeting had finished. Then he spoke into the phone. "Jamie, don't leave town. I have reason to believe someone is after you. Get in touch with me right away, and please come to my house."

The worried look on his face as he disconnected the call made Jessica's breath catch. "I'm sorry you couldn't reach him. Is there anything I can do to help?"

He shook his head. "No. But whatever Jamie has gotten himself involved in seems to have spilled over into your life, too. I'm sorry about that."

"Don't be. I'm glad I was there today to keep him from being killed."

His eyes softened, and he smiled. "I am, too. I always said you were the best cop I ever worked with. It's good to see that you haven't lost your edge."

"Thanks, Ryan. I'm glad we've talked tonight even if it's turned into concern for your brother. Please let me know if you hear from him. Now, why don't you go on home and get some rest so you can be at the top of your game tomorrow."

"I will." He paused and glanced around the apartment. "But what about you? Do you think you'll be all right here by yourself?"

She chuckled. "I've been taking care of myself for a long time. I'll be fine."

He cocked an eyebrow and stared at her. "The last time I was here was because of a break-in. What's to say it won't happen again?"

"I've got new locks now and a new security system. Robbers could probably break into a bank easier than they could get in here. Don't worry. I'll be fine."

"I don't know. Maybe you should go to Adam's house for the night."

"Adam and Claire are out of town for a few days. I'm better off here. Now, go on and don't worry about me."

She turned and walked toward the door with him right behind. He stopped when she opened the door. "Keep your gun close and call me if you have any problems."

"I will."

He stepped into the hallway and turned back to her. "Also, don't forget about coming to the precinct tomorrow to look at some mug shots. Maybe you can spot the gunman."

"I'll be there. How about ten o'clock?"

"That will work. I'll see you then." He didn't move to leave. Instead, his gaze drifted over her face. "Thank you, Jessica, for listening to me tonight. Think about what I've said. I hope it will help to change your opinion of what kind of man I am. I really want us to be friends again."

"You've given me a lot to think about. I'll see you in the morning."

He nodded. "See you then."

Before he could say more, she closed the door and locked the dead bolt. Then she walked into the kitchen and checked to see if she'd locked the back door securely when she came in. Satisfied that she was safe inside, she set the security system.

She knew she should eat something but she wasn't hungry. All she wanted was to go to bed and try to forget all that had happened today. With a sigh she headed for her bedroom.

Twenty minutes later, she lay in bed, her gun and her cell phone on the bedside table beside the landline she still had. Adam had teased her about the added

expense, but she liked having the familiar phone she'd
had in her bedroom at home when she was growing
up. Somehow it reminded her of happier times, when
her father would yell at her to get off the phone, or
she and Claire would talk for hours about which boys
from school they were going to marry.

She sighed and pounded her pillow. Now Claire was
her sister-in-law, married to Jessica's older brother,
but there was no hope for romance in her own life.
She'd had her heart broken once, and she didn't want
to chance it happening again. It was better if she just
concentrated on her job and building a life for herself
and ignored the loneliness that plagued her.

Her eyes drifted shut, and she was almost asleep
when she awoke to the sound of a ringing telephone.
For a moment she thought it was her cell phone, but
then she realized it was the landline.

She fumbled for the switch on the lamp by the
phone and turned it on. Then she grabbed the receiver
and pushed up in bed. "Hello." The word sounded
hoarse, and she tried again. "Hello."

"Good evening, Miss Knight. How are you?"

She sat up straighter and frowned. "Who is this?"

"It's a friend you met earlier today."

Although the voice was friendly, she knew the
caller was not. "Oh, it's you," she said. "What do you
want?"

He chuckled. "Right to the point, aren't you? What
do I want? Oh, nothing at the present time. If I decide
I want anything from you, you'll know it. Now, have
a good night's sleep."

Jessica stared at the phone as the call disconnected.
Without hesitation she pushed Redial and waited for

the call to go through. Instead, a high, piercing tone stabbed at her ear. "The last call is not accessible from this phone," an automated voice said.

She punched the end button and put the phone back on the hook. After a moment, she reached over and disconnected the phone from the wall. At least she wouldn't have to worry about him calling again tonight unless he had her cell phone number. She doubted he did, but he probably did know where she lived.

She grabbed her gun and climbed out of bed. It was no use. She wasn't going to get any sleep, which was probably what her caller had intended in the first place.

The memory of the robber's face flashed into her head. He might know her and where she lived, but she knew what he looked like. And that was going to come in quite handy when she examined those mug shots tomorrow.

If his picture was there, she'd find him, and then it would only be a matter of time before the police found him.

Ryan glanced over at his partner, Detective Mac Barnes, and arched his eyebrows. "What are you staring at?"

Mac chuckled and shook his head before he looked down at the file on his desk. "Nothing. I've just never seen you so worried about housekeeping as you've been this morning. You've not only organized that mess you call a desk, but you've dusted it and the chairs. Even made a fresh pot of coffee. Who're we expecting? The first lady?"

Ryan's face warmed, and he busied himself straightening the books on the shelf behind his desk. "Cut it out, Mac. I thought it was time we made this office a bit more presentable. What if the DA or the police commissioner came in here? You'd want it cleaned up, wouldn't you?"

Mac's eyes sparkled, and he tried to suppress the smile pulling at his lips. "Yeah, I expect we'd better get ready if the commissioner's coming."

Ryan huffed and sat down in his desk chair. "I didn't say he was coming, but he could." He glanced around the office. "Anyway, it looks better now than it did when I came in this morning."

Mac just shook his head and turned his attention back to the report he'd been working on since arriving for work. Ryan glanced at the clock and frowned. It was after ten, and Jessica still hadn't arrived. He hadn't felt good about leaving her last night, but she'd insisted she'd be fine. What if she wasn't, though?

He pulled his cell phone out and checked for text messages again, but nothing had come in. Not from Jessica, and not from Jamie. He'd been calling and texting his brother all night, to no avail. Still, he typed out another message asking Jamie to call and hit Send. He could only hope his brother would respond.

A knock at the door interrupted his thoughts and he jumped to his feet. "I'll get it."

Mac looked up, a surprised expression on his face. "Okay."

Ryan pulled the door open and smiled in relief at the sight of Jessica standing in the hallway. "I was beginning to worry. It's after ten. I thought something might have happened."

She shook her head. "I'm fine. Adam called this morning, and we talked longer than I thought. I'm sorry I'm late."

"Late for what?" Mac's voice behind him startled Ryan, and he glanced around at his partner. Before Ryan could say anything, Mac pushed past him and grabbed Jessica in a bear hug. "Jessica! It's good to see you. What are you doing here?"

She returned Mac's hug and smiled. "Didn't Ryan tell you? I'm supposed to look at mug shots today."

Mac swung his gaze around to Ryan and grinned. "Oh, and I thought the first lady was coming."

A puzzled look flashed across Jessica's face. "What do you mean?"

Mac shook his head, grabbed Jessica's arm and pulled her into the office. "It's nothing. Ryan's been cleaning all morning. I thought we had important company coming." He grinned down at her and chucked her under the chin. "Of course, if I'd known you were the one he expected, I would have been right in there helping get ready. It's always good to see you."

She sat down in the chair by Ryan's desk and let her gaze drift around the room. "This is the first time I've been back since I transferred out. Everything looks the same, though."

Mac patted his stomach and grinned. "Well, it's not all the same. Some of us have put on weight." He glanced at Ryan. "And some of us can eat anything they want and never gain an ounce."

Ryan joined in the laughter. Then he grew more serious and sat down on the edge of his desk. "I told Mac about the robbery yesterday."

Mac nodded. "Yeah, but you didn't give me the details. What happened, Jessica?"

Ryan watched her face as she told his partner about the incident in the convenience store. As she spoke, concern for his brother grew. Why hadn't Jamie called back?

After she'd finished, Mac pursed his lips and didn't say anything for a moment. Then he exhaled. "I think you're probably right about it being a setup to kill Jamie. The question, though, is why." He turned to Ryan. "Does he go there often?"

Ryan nodded. "It's near his campus, and he's told me he goes by there every afternoon to get a cup of coffee before he goes to work at the computer store. Jamie is a creature of habit, so it wouldn't be hard for someone to track him. He doesn't deviate from his routine very often."

"Except now," Jessica said. "He's deviated quite a bit by suddenly disappearing and not letting anyone know where he is."

Ryan rubbed the back of his neck. "You're right about that. I still haven't heard from him. I intend to let him have it when he comes home."

Before either Jessica or Mac could speak, a knock sounded at the door. Ryan opened it to find one of the department clerks holding a manila envelope in her hand.

"The lab sent these reports over to you. It's from that robbery at the convenience store yesterday."

"Good. Thank you for bringing it to us."

He brought the envelope back to his desk and opened it. He pulled out several sheets of paper. Mac stepped up beside him, and Ryan held the reports so that Mac could read along with him.

After he read the first few lines, Ryan had to take a deep breath to slow his accelerated heartbeat. He glanced at Mac, who frowned in concentration as he scrutinized the lab's findings. Ryan directed his attention back to the report and didn't look up again until he'd read the final word.

For a moment neither of them spoke. Then Mac gave a soft whistle. "I never expected that."

"Me neither," Ryan said.

Jessica, who'd been silent while they were reading, rose from her chair. "I know I'm not a police officer anymore, but I'd really like to know what the lab discovered. Can you tell me?"

Ryan and Mac exchanged glances before Ryan nodded. "I think this may involve you as much as anybody else."

She cocked her head to one side and stared at him. "How do you figure that?"

He looked down at the report again. "The lab found a fingerprint on the gun, and they've identified it as belonging to a man named Lee Tucker. He's been arrested before, and his fingerprints as well as his DNA are in the system. In fact, there's an arrest warrant out on him right now for attempted murder. He was arrested but skipped bail."

Jessica's eyebrows arched. "Skipped bail, huh? I wonder why we haven't found out about him at the Knight Agency."

Ryan handed her one of the pages from the envelope. "They sent a picture of his mug shot along with the report. He seems to fit the description you gave of the robber, but we need you to make a positive identification. Is this the man you shot at the convenience store yesterday?"

Jessica took the picture in her hand and studied it for a moment before she handed it back to him. "Yes, this is the same man. I'm sure of it."

Ryan slipped the photo back into the stack of papers. "Then you met Lee Tucker in the flesh at that store."

"But I don't understand. You made it sound like I was involved in some other way than being able to identify this guy. What did you mean?"

"There was some blood on the gun."

She nodded. "From the wound where I shot him."

"Yes. Just a small spot, but it was enough to get a DNA sample. It was also a match to Tucker. So we have his fingerprint and his DNA on the weapon he used to try to kill Jamie."

"I still don't see—"

"There's more," Ryan said. "Remember the case we were working together when I asked for a transfer to another partner?"

"Yes. Cal and Susan Harvey were investigative reporters who were found murdered in their midtown Memphis home. They'd been working on a story about the drug trade in the South."

"And there was a bandana with gang symbols on it found in their home," Ryan finished for her. "And an anonymous tip informed the police that the bandana belonged to Tommie Oakes, a gang member who went by the name of Cruiser. We found the murder weapon in his closet."

Jessica nodded as she no doubt recalled the case

that had caused such a rift between the two of them. She took a deep breath. "Although his DNA was on the bandana, he had an alibi that the police and the DA ignored. They argued that the DNA on the gun probably belonged to another gang member who wasn't in the system. Your new partner at the time couldn't wait to close the case, and he kept on until the DA had Oakes arrested and charged. He was convicted and is now serving a life sentence in prison."

"That's right."

"So why are we rehashing this now?" Jessica said through gritted teeth.

"Because the DNA found on the gun that killed the Harveys has been in the system ever since. The lab sent the DNA from the convenience-store robbery to the database, and it matched the results from the Harvey case."

Jessica's eyes grew wide. "So if the DNA from yesterday's robbery is Lee Tucker's, then he must have been the person who shot the Harveys." She shook her head. "But the evidence from the Harvey case has been in the system for four years. Why didn't it show a hit on Lee Tucker before now?"

Ryan shrugged. "The lab people don't know. The important thing is that it does now. Tucker had to be at the Harveys' home the night they were killed."

"So Oakes might not have been the killer."

He nodded. "Maybe not. The real killer could be—"

"Lee Tucker." Her expression changed instantly. Alarm took over her features as she no doubt realized the danger that he had come to understand moments ago. "The police have to stop Tucker before he follows through and kills Jamie, too."

"I know," Ryan said. He tried to keep his anxiety reined in.

"But Lee Tucker could be anywhere," Jessica said. "How would you decide where to start looking?"

Ryan held up one of the papers from the report. "I think we start with the car that you saw leave the scene after the shooting yesterday. The license plate is registered to the reelection campaign of Hayden Mitchum."

Jessica's eyes grew wide. "The US senator?"

Ryan nodded. "Yes. When we called his reelection headquarters this morning, they said they hadn't realized it was missing. It's one of the cars that the senator's aide uses when he's in town, but he is in Washington right now with Senator Mitchum."

The phone on Mac's desk rang at that moment, and Mac answered. "Detective Barnes."

Ryan waited until Mac hung up before he said anything else. "Do we need to answer a call?"

Mac shook his head. "No. That was the captain. He needs me to bring him up to speed on the investigation into Gerald Price's murder."

"I read about that," Jessica said. "He's the man whose body was found in a riverfront parking lot. The newspaper report said the police believe he was killed in a carjacking."

"That's right." Mac turned to Ryan. "I can go over everything with the captain. You stay here and talk to Jessica." He reached over and patted her on the shoulder. "It's good to see you. I hope you'll come back to visit soon."

She smiled. "Maybe I will, Mac. Take care of yourself out there."

He nodded and walked from the room. Ryan waited until Mac had closed the door behind him before he spoke.

He stuck his hands in his pockets and took a deep breath. "Jessica, yesterday I thought I was going to a store to make sure my brother was okay. Since then, what was thought to be a robbery has snowballed into something that appears to be much deeper. And somehow it has ties to the murders we investigated four years ago."

"I know," she murmured as if she was lost in thought.

He sat down on the edge of his desk again and faced Jessica, who took the opposite chair. "What is Lee Tucker's connection to the murders of two reporters four years ago and to what appeared to be a random robbery yesterday? And why was the getaway car stolen from a US senator's parking lot? It doesn't make sense."

She nodded in agreement, then added, "If it really was stolen."

"That's a possibility. The senator's office could have been lying about that." He stood up, paced to the far side of the office and came back to sit in front of her. "And why did my brother suddenly disappear?"

"And why did I receive a threatening telephone call?"

Now it was his turn to be startled. "When did that happen?"

She shrugged. "Last night. A man called I think just to scare me so I couldn't sleep. I have to say it worked."

"What did he say?"

"When I asked who was calling, he said it was the

friend I met earlier. So it must have been Lee Tucker," Jessica answered. "I asked him what he wanted, and he said he didn't want anything at the present time. But he'd let me know if he changed his mind."

Ryan pounded his fist down on his desk. "That settles it. I have to find out what's going on."

"How are you going to do that?" she asked.

He thought for a moment before he responded. "I think I'll take a few days' leave and poke around on my own to see what I can find out. Maybe I can turn up something."

She pushed out of her chair. "Well, I wish you luck. Let me know if I can help in any way."

He stood and faced her. "You can. How about working with me for a few days? Let's see if we can find out what's going on."

She stared at him as if he'd lost his mind. "You can't be serious."

"I am. After all, Lee Tucker is a fugitive and you're a bounty hunter. If we find him, maybe we can answer some questions we've always had about Cal's and Susan Harvey's murders. And you may get to bring in a fugitive who's skipped bail."

She stared into his eyes without blinking. "Ryan, I don't know…"

He reached for her hand and clasped it in his. "Please, Jessica. It'll be like old times. The two of us working on a case. What do you say? Want to be my partner again?"

FOUR

Jessica swallowed the last bite of her hamburger and took a sip of iced tea before glancing across the table at Ryan. She still couldn't believe this was happening. Twenty-four hours ago no one could have convinced her that she would be having lunch today with Ryan Spencer. And yet here she was, sitting across from the man she'd told herself for four years that she hoped she would never see again.

As they had discussed the Harvey murder case and its link to the robbery and what was believed to be an attempt on Jamie's life yesterday, she had found herself feeling comfortable in Ryan's presence. Maybe she had been too quick to jump to conclusions four years ago. In all honesty, he had tried to explain his side back then, but she had felt so betrayed that she wouldn't listen. Her brothers had always said she had a stubborn side to her sweet personality. No wonder Ryan had given up on trying to convince her she was wrong.

On the other hand, he'd had four years. Why had he waited until last night to try again to convince her?

"What are you thinking?" Ryan's voice cut into her thoughts, and she sat up straighter.

Her face grew warm, and she picked up her napkin and wiped her mouth. "Oh, just lost in thought, I guess."

A skeptical look flashed in his eyes, and he regarded her with an arched eyebrow. "Come on, Jessica. I always told you that your face was like a mirror to your soul. You never have been able to hide your emotions. Is it me? Are you still trying to make up your mind about whether or not you can be my friend?"

There was no use evading the truth. He was right. He'd always been able to read the expressions on her face. Maybe that was what had made them such great partners. The thought of their former relationship and how it had ended sent her heart plummeting to the pit of her stomach. Could she really put the past behind her and be his friend? And could she really work with him on a case?

She took a deep breath and tried to smile. "I listened to all you said last night, and I wish I had done that long ago. I didn't, and I've had four years to ponder everything that was said between us."

He chuckled and shook his head. "Still the same old Jessica, huh? Once you get something in your mind, you're like a dog with a bone. You chew on it constantly, and the longer you do, the more you take ownership of it." He leaned forward and clasped her hand on the tabletop. "I've told you the truth about what was going on with me then. I'm sorry that I didn't handle things differently, and I'm sorry I hurt you. Why don't you quit stewing about it and bury that bone. All I'm asking is to be your friend."

She started to pull her hand free, but he tightened his grip. A tug-of-war was the last thing she wanted in the middle of a downtown restaurant, so she relaxed. Maybe Ryan was right. Maybe her brothers had been right, too, about her stubborn streak when it came to forgiving those who she felt had hurt her. And Ryan had fit into that category…until their talk last night. Now she was beginning to think she'd jumped to conclusions before she should have.

After a moment, she smiled. "I'd like us to be friends again, Ryan. I always enjoyed working with you."

"And I liked it, too. I was really sorry when I heard you had left the department." He released her hand, and she picked up her iced tea again. "Maybe if I had been more forthcoming about what was going on in my life then, you might still be a police officer."

She took a drink from her glass and shook her head. "I don't think so. All my family has ever known is the bounty-hunter business. It was just a matter of time before I joined my brothers at the agency."

He tilted his head to one side and studied her. "Are you happy doing that kind of work? It sounds like it would be dangerous for a woman to take down guys determined not to go to jail."

"That doesn't sound a lot different from what I did as a police officer. But I'm careful, and I don't take chances. I'm on the road a lot, so the job's not conducive to much of a personal life. And I get tired of staying in motels and eating in restaurants."

He smiled. "That must be hard for you. I remember how you used to talk about the kind of house you wanted and what the backyard would be like. You haven't found the right one yet?"

She shook her head and sighed. "No. Maybe someday. What about you? You said you moved into the house your dad bought before his death. Do you still live there?"

"Yeah. All by myself now." He chuckled and wiped at the condensation on the outside of his iced tea glass. "Of course, as soon as Jamie got to college he wanted to move into an apartment of his own near campus. So I'm left rambling around in a big house all by myself. I'm thinking of selling it and moving back to an apartment." He paused and bit down on his lip.

Jessica pushed her plate out of the way and crossed her arms on the table in front of her. "What's the matter?"

"I'm sitting here talking about my housing plans when I should be trying to find out where my brother has gone." He pushed back the hair that had fallen across his forehead. "I can't believe he wouldn't tell me."

Jessica sat still for a moment and studied Ryan. When she had last known Ryan, he was working to establish a good relationship with his brother. From the way they'd seemed yesterday, she suspected they'd been able to do that. If that was so, why had Jamie left town without letting Ryan know where he was going?

She picked up her napkin again and wiped her hands. "Do you know any of the people Jamie works with at the computer store or at the school newspaper?"

"Nobody at the computer store, but I met the student editor once when I stopped by the newspaper office. Why?"

"I was just thinking," she said. "Maybe we could talk to someone at the paper and see if they could help us."

Ryan nodded. "I think that's a good idea. I'll call and see if anybody's there."

He pulled his cell phone from his pocket and scrolled down to a number. The muscle in his jaw flexed as he waited. After a moment, he ended the call. "Nobody answered. They may all be in class or at lunch."

"Why don't we go over to the campus anyway. We might find someone in the building who could tell us when they'll be back."

Ryan smiled and glanced down at her plate. "If you're through, I'll get the check so we can go."

He picked up the tab the waitress had laid on the table and pushed to his feet. A panicked shock ricocheted through her body. No, she couldn't allow herself to let down her guard with Ryan. She didn't mind helping him find his brother, but they weren't about to renew the relationship they'd had before. Jessica put out a hand to stop him. "I'll pay for my lunch, Ryan."

"There's no need for that. You're helping me. The least I can do is buy you some lunch."

She shook her head and rose to her feet. "No. I think it would be better if we keep this new partnership as professional as possible."

He narrowed his eyes and studied her suspiciously. "What are you getting at, Jessica?"

"I'm saying I don't want you buying me lunch or dinner or anything else. I can take care of my own meals. Let's just keep things on a professional basis."

Ryan exhaled a soft breath. "Okay, Jessica, if that's the way you want it."

She bobbed her head in a curt nod. "That's the way I want it."

He gritted his teeth. "All right, then. I'll have the cashier divide the tab. Is that agreeable?"

"That will be fine."

Muttering under his breath, he whirled and strode toward the cashier. As she followed along, she strained to hear what he was saying but could catch only a few words. "Women…unreasonable…holding a grudge."

She stopped halfway to the cashier and stared at Ryan's back. Was she being unreasonable, and was she holding on to a grudge? She tried to shake the guilty thoughts from her head.

He seemed sincere about wanting her to forgive him. If so, she needed to meet him halfway and try to put past hurts out of her mind. The memory of how they'd taken turns paying for each other's food when they were partners popped into her mind, and she hurried to catch up with him. She caught him right before he got to the cash register.

"Ryan, wait a minute."

He turned and cocked an eyebrow. "What is it?"

"I'm sorry if I sounded too negative. I suppose I thought your offer appeared to be a bit too personal at first."

His eyes darkened. "I'm sorry, Jessica. I didn't mean to make you feel uncomfortable. I'm just so glad to be having lunch with you again after all these years that I guess I forgot you still don't completely trust me."

"Please, Ryan, let's not make a big deal out of it. Why don't we do what we used to. We take turns picking up the tab. Is that all right?"

"That sounds good." He held out the bill and grinned. "Do you want to take the first one?"

She stared at his outstretched hand for a moment

and then burst out laughing before she jerked the tab from him. "I guess I asked for that."

He slipped his hands into his pockets and rocked back on his heels. A teasing gleam lit his eyes. "I guess you did. I'll get the car and bring it around front while you pay the bill. See you in a few minutes."

Jessica shook her head as Ryan walked out of the restaurant. She'd forgotten how much she used to enjoy being with him. Was it possible they could be friends after all that had happened between them? She hadn't thought so a few days ago, but now she wasn't so sure.

She sighed and shook her head. There'd be time later for thoughts like that. Right now the most important thing was to find out why Lee Tucker had tried to kill Jamie yesterday and why Jamie had disappeared without letting his brother know where he was going.

When those questions were answered, she would make a decision on remaining friends with Ryan.

Ryan led the way down the hallway of the building that housed the college newspaper's office. Jessica walked beside him, and he glanced at her every once in a while as if to assure himself that she was really there.

He'd missed her these past few years, more than he would ever admit to her. There was no telling how many times he'd wished he could talk with her about a case he was working on. It seemed she'd always had an insight that had helped unravel what had seemed a mystery to him.

But most of all, he'd missed the quiet times they'd spent together, talking about their families and sharing their hopes for the future. He'd always envied her close relationship with her brothers. Perhaps that was what had made his with Jamie so difficult. He hadn't known how to cope with a teenager's problems, and he'd missed Jessica's advice during those years.

When he looked back on what had happened between them, he realized he'd handled it all wrong. She had been the perfect person who could have helped him through what he now recognized as a period of depression in his life. But instead of leaning on her, he'd turned his back on her.

It had come as a complete surprise when she'd been transferred instead of him. No matter how much he'd tried to explain, she wouldn't listen. And he had missed their times together ever since. Maybe they'd never share what they had once had, but at least she was talking to him now. And she was helping him.

"I see the *Panther*'s office ahead."

Her voice jerked him from his thoughts, and he stared at the sign identifying the offices of the school's student newspaper above a door down the hall. When they arrived at the spot, he was surprised to find the door open. Inside, a young woman sat at a desk, a computer in front of her.

She looked up when they walked in and darted a glance at each of them before she rose to her feet. "Hello. Can I help you with something?"

"I hope so," Ryan said. "I'm Ryan Spencer, Jamie's brother."

Her eyes lit up and she came around the desk toward them. "It's so nice to meet you. I'm Ellie Howington, one of the staff reporters. Jamie and I work together, and I've heard a lot about you. It's nice to meet you at last."

"You, too. I wonder if you could help me out."

Her eyes widened with what he thought was fear, and she glanced from him to Jessica. Her lips quivered. "Is it Jamie? Has something happened?"

"Oh, no," he said. "I just have a few questions to ask."

She breathed an audible sigh of relief and closed her eyes for a moment. "Oh, good. You scared me for a moment there."

The girl's reaction wasn't what Ryan would have expected from someone who just worked with his brother. And then there had been her statement she was glad to meet him *at last*. Perhaps there was more to Jamie and Ellie's relationship than merely colleagues on the newspaper. Ryan cocked his head to one side and stared at her.

"Why would you think something might have happened to Jamie?"

Ellie's face flushed, and she pointed at a dilapidated sofa across the room. "Why don't we sit down. We have a few minutes before anyone will be back from class."

Ryan and Jessica walked over to the couch, sat down and waited for Ellie to drag over a chair from the other side of the room. When she was settled across from them, Ryan scooted to the edge of his seat and rested his elbows on his knees. "Is there something I need to know?"

Ellie bit down on her lip and nodded. "Jamie and I have worked together for about a year on the newspaper. We got on so well together that about six months ago we began to go out. At first it was maybe a night a week, but as time went by, we spent more and more time together. Now we're together every spare minute."

Ryan's body stiffened, and a stab of disappointment jabbed at his heart. Jamie had never said a word to him about a special girl in his life. Ryan rubbed his hand across his forehead and frowned. "Why hasn't Jamie told me about this?"

Ellie shrugged. "This feeling between us is so new that we didn't want to share it with anyone yet. We'd decided, though, that this weekend Jamie would ask you out to dinner so that you and I could meet." Her eyes filled with tears. "Now I don't think we'll be able to do that. Jamie's gone, and I don't know where he is."

Those weren't the words he'd hoped to hear at the newspaper office. "Yes, I know," Ryan said. "I'd hoped someone here would be able to tell me where he's gone."

Ellie shook her head. "I wish I knew. He came by my apartment last night and told me what happened in the convenience store yesterday. He said he knew the robber had meant to kill him, and he knew why."

Ryan shot a glance at Jessica. "Did he tell you what that reason was?"

"He said it was about the story he was working on."

Ryan repressed the groan that he felt rising in his throat. So Jamie had gotten into some news story that had placed him in jeopardy. "What is the story about?"

Ellie held up her hands in a gesture of helplessness. "It was just supposed to be about the candidates running for office. That's all. But it turned into something more."

"What candidates? What office?"

Ellie started to speak, but before she did, she looked over her shoulder at the open door and rose from her chair. She hurried across the room and closed the door then returned to them. When she was seated again, she clasped her hands in her lap and glanced from Jessica to him.

"I suppose you've been following the US Senate race?"

Jessica and Ryan both nodded. Then Jessica leaned forward a bit. "You said Jamie was working on a story about the candidates. Who was he supposed to interview? Chip Holder or Senator Mitchum?"

"Actually, it wasn't an interview, although he hoped it would turn into one. His first step was to attend the debate they had. You know that Chip Holder is a decorated war hero, and he's been running some ads that accuse Senator Mitchum of having lots of skeletons in his closet."

"I've seen some of them," Ryan said. "Holder seems to have a slight edge over Senator Mitchum at the moment. His experiences as a POW of a terrorist group in the Middle East and his rescue six years ago by a Special Ops group have given him a lot of material to wow the American voters with. The media have painted him as a real patriot who served his country in the worst of circumstances, and the public seems to like that."

"Plus the fact," Jessica said, "that he's a young, good-looking man with an outgoing personality. He's running on his war record and promises to bring our troops home from overseas and put an end to the ongoing conflict in the Middle East."

Ryan nodded. "On the other hand, we have Senator Mitchum, who has been in office for twelve years and is highly respected in Washington. He's on the Armed Services Committee that deals with matters related to the common defense. He has a great record in the Senate. From what I've read, though, neither of the candidates cares for the other one. I saw their debate last week on TV. They had some heated exchanges."

"That's the debate Jamie attended, and that's what he said," Ellie added. "It seemed that accusations were thrown out on both sides, and neither could prove what they were saying." Ellie took a deep breath and leaned forward. "But something else happened that night."

Ryan's eyebrows arched. "What?"

"When Jamie was leaving the debate, he saw a man in the parking lot whose car wouldn't start. Jamie went over to see if he could help, and the man said he thought it was his battery. Jamie had some jumper cables in his car, and he helped the man get his car started. Then the guy asked Jamie to go for coffee as a thank-you for helping him. They ended up at an all-night restaurant and talked until the wee hours."

Ryan darted a glance at Jessica and then back to Ellie. "Did he say who this guy was?"

"Yes. He said the man claimed to be an investigative reporter and that he was working on a story, but somehow Jamie didn't believe him. He couldn't quite figure out why, but he thought the reporter label was just a cover."

"Cover for what?"

Ellie shrugged. "He didn't know, but he said the guy was friendly and talked a lot about stories he'd written over the years. Jamie hadn't heard of any of them and had decided the man was making up a lot of it. But he listened until he finally decided it was time to go. As he stood to leave, he reached across the table to shake hands and accidentally knocked the man's briefcase to the floor. It opened, and papers fell out everywhere. Jamie was so embarrassed, and he squatted down and began picking up papers. Then he saw one that made him pause."

"What was it?" Ryan asked.

"There were some pages stapled together with a newspaper clipping about the murders of Cal and Susan Harvey."

"Cal and Susan Harvey?" Ryan and Jessica said at the same time.

"Yes. Jamie thought the names were familiar, and he picked the papers up and asked the man if that was the story he was working on. Jamie said the guy became really agitated and jerked the papers out of his hand. Then he stuffed everything into his briefcase and said he had to go. Jamie couldn't get the names out of his mind, and when he got home, he started searching the internet. That's when he found out that you, Ryan, had investigated that case."

Ryan sat up straighter and frowned. "But he didn't mention it to me."

"I know. He was going to, but then a few days later he read in the paper that there had been a body found in a riverfront parking lot. There was a picture of the victim, and Jamie recognized him. It was

Gerald Price, the man he'd had coffee with. He knew there was a story there, and he decided to find out what it was."

Ryan raked his hand through his hair. "That crazy kid. Why didn't he tell me all this?"

"I told him to do that, but he said you'd be upset with him. He wanted to prove he could do something on his own. And when he told me he was going to Nashville last Saturday to do some research on his story, I begged him to tell you, but he wouldn't."

"Do you know where he went in Nashville?"

Ellie shook her head. "He was very secretive when he came back, but he seemed to be brooding about something. Then on Wednesday he told me he was going to go to both candidates' campaign offices and see if he could get interviews."

"And did he?" Ryan asked.

She shrugged. "I don't know. I didn't hear from him again until yesterday, when he came by here before he headed to the computer store to work. He said he'd found out something that changed everything."

"What was it?" Jessica asked.

"I asked him that, and he said he didn't want to say anything else until he was certain. Then he said he had to get to work, and he left. Later he came by my apartment to tell me what happened at the convenience store and that he was going out of town for a few days. He asked me to cover for him at the paper."

"And he didn't tell you where he was going?" Ryan asked again.

Tears pooled in Ellie's eyes. "No, and I'm worried sick about him. I haven't heard a word. I've been leaving messages for him, but he hasn't returned any of my calls." She paused for a moment and brushed at the tears that were spilling down her cheeks. "Do you have any idea where he could be, Ryan?"

Ryan exhaled a long breath and pushed to his feet. "I don't know, but if I hear from him, I'll let you know." He reached in his pocket, pulled out his card and handed it to Ellie. "Here's my number. If you hear anything, you let me know right away. Okay?"

Ellie took the card, sniffed and stood. "I will."

Ryan glanced around at Jessica, who was standing beside him. "I think we'd better go now and see if we can figure out what's going on with that brother of mine." He turned back to Ellie and grasped her hand. "It's good to meet you, Ellie. When Jamie gets back, I'm going to let him have it for keeping you a secret from me."

She smiled, and her eyes sparkled with tears. "Thank you, Ryan. It was great meeting you." She nodded to Jessica. "And you, too."

Jessica reached out and touched Ellie's arm. "Don't worry. Jamie will be fine."

"I hope you're right," she said.

A few minutes later, Ryan and Jessica emerged from the building into the sunshine, and he stopped to face her. "Can you believe this? Jamie has gotten himself involved in something that has to do with the Cal and Susan Harvey case."

Jessica nodded. "I know. I wonder if he remembered the victims' names because he heard you talk about them."

"I don't know. But there's one thing I do know. I never felt good about Tommie Oakes being convicted of that crime. It's beginning to look like there may have been more to it after all."

Jessica didn't say anything for a moment but seemed to be lost in thought. After a moment, she took a breath. "What should we do now?"

"You mentioned that you thought the clerk at the store might have been in on the attempt on Jamie's life. Why don't we go talk to him."

"Okay. Are we going to the store or to his place?"

Ryan pulled out his phone. "I'll call the station and get the numbers for both, and the guy's home address from the police report."

A few minutes later, they were back at the car. Ryan had made the call to the convenience store, but the clerk wasn't working today. "Let's drop by his house and see if he's home."

As Ryan guided the car away from the curb, he gripped the steering wheel harder to steady his shaking fingers. He couldn't help feeling frightened for his brother. If Jamie had become involved in a murder case where justice had not been served, then that meant the Harveys' killer was still at large. He'd killed two seasoned investigative reporters and he certainly wouldn't stop at doing the same to a young college-newspaper reporter.

Ryan had to find Jamie, and fast.

FIVE

When they stopped outside the apartment building where Richard Parker lived, Jessica glanced over at Ryan. He hadn't said much on the ride here from the college, and she wondered if the conversation with Ellie had upset him.

His hands still rested on the steering wheel, and she reached over and grasped his arm. "Are you okay, Ryan?"

He glanced down at her hand before he looked up into her face and smiled. His eyes, however, still held the troubled look she remembered when he would be concerned over a case they were working. "I'm scared of what Jamie's gotten himself into and a bit surprised that he kept his relationship with Ellie a secret from me. But then, I never have been able to figure that kid out. He jumps into things before he has time to think."

"Not like his big brother, who has to study every little detail before he makes a decision." She couldn't help but smile at the surprised look that flashed across his face.

"Is that what I do? I thought I was just being careful, always trying to do the right thing." His eyebrows pulled together in a frown. "I made the wrong decision when it came to our relationship, though, didn't I? I decided to act alone instead of talking it out with you and telling you how I was really feeling. I'm sorry now I didn't do that."

Jessica cleared her throat and reached to unfasten her seat belt. "Maybe you've learned from that, Ryan. From the short time I talked with Jamie yesterday, I found him to be a sensible young man. That didn't just happen. You helped him develop into the person he is. I'm sure he's learned enough from you that he'll be careful no matter where he is or what he's doing."

"I hope you're right." He looked past her to the apartment building. "This is the address Mac gave me from the police report. Are you ready to go and question Richard?"

"I am."

As they walked toward the entrance, Jessica couldn't help but have a feeling of déjà vu. How many times in the past had she and Ryan walked side by side on their way to question a suspect or a witness to a crime?

Being a bounty hunter at times could be a lonely job and it could be dangerous if a fugitive was approached in the wrong way, especially if there was no backup. But she and Ryan had always worked well together, and she had to admit it felt right, comfortable to be back with him now.

They walked into the lobby of the apartment building, and Ryan pointed to the elevator. "Mac said he's in apartment 201. That's on the second floor."

Jessica cast a teasing look at him. "Getting too soft for the stairs, Spencer?"

He grinned at the ongoing joke they had enjoyed when they worked together and shook his head. "I can still keep up with you any day, Knight."

They both laughed and headed for the stairs. As they climbed up to the second-floor landing, Jessica smiled to herself. Maybe she and Ryan could find their way to being friends after all.

They stepped into the hallway of the second floor and stared at the doors that lined each side. About halfway down, Jessica spotted a young man knocking on an apartment door. As they approached, she could see that a frown covered his face. He pounded on the door again and yelled out. "Hey, Parker, are you in there?"

She and Ryan stopped beside him, outside apartment 201, and Ryan pulled his badge from his pocket. "I'm Detective Ryan Spencer. We're looking for Richard Parker."

The young man's eyes grew wide as he stared at the badge and then he nodded. "This is his apartment. He's supposed to drive me to work, but I can't get him to answer the door."

"Have you spoken with him today?" Ryan asked.

"Yes, about eight this morning. I told him I was having car trouble, and he said it was no problem for him to drive me. But now I can't get him to answer the door or the phone. I thought maybe he had gone out, but I checked and his car is in the parking lot."

Ryan stepped around the young man. "Let me try." He raised his hand and banged on the door. "Richard, this is Detective Ryan Spencer. If you're in there, open the door for us."

No sound came from behind the door.

Jessica moved to stand beside Ryan. "Do you think we need to try to get in?"

"I think so." He turned to the young man. "Can you go and get the superintendent to open this door. It's possible that Richard is sick or hurt. We need to get in and check on him."

He was turning and running down the hall before Ryan had finished speaking. He looked over his shoulder and called out, "I'll be right back."

Jessica watched him go before she looked back at Ryan. "I don't like this."

Ryan's mouth puckered in a grim line. "Neither do I."

Within minutes, the young neighbor reappeared with the building superintendent right behind. The man wore a work belt with various tools hanging from it, and he reached for a big ring of keys that jangled against his leg.

He stopped in front of Ryan and stared at him. "I'm the super here. Are you the police officer wanting to get into Richard's apartment?"

Ryan nodded and pulled his jacket back to reveal his badge at his belt. "I'm Detective Ryan Spencer, and this is Jessica Knight. We're trying to locate a missing person and need to talk to Richard. He hasn't come to the door and his friend here tells me he's not answering his phone. We need to make sure he's okay."

The man nodded, inserted the key in the door and pushed it open. He took a half step inside the apartment. "Richard, are you in here?"

There was no answer.

His senses no doubt on alert, Ryan moved around

the superintendent, pulled his gun and held it in front of him as he stepped into a small hallway that led into a room at the far end. Jessica followed close behind. She strained to hear a sound, any sound, but there was only silence.

Ahead of her, Ryan reached the end of the hall and turned toward the left and the room that lay beyond. Suddenly he stopped, and she'd been following so closely she bumped into his back. She heard Ryan's sharp inhalation of breath.

"What is it?" she whispered.

"It's Richard Parker."

He moved aside enough so that Jessica could step up beside him. Her eyes grew wide, and she gasped at the sight before her. Richard Parker, his open and unseeing eyes staring upward, lay in a pool of blood on his living room floor.

Jessica pulled her gun and glanced at Ryan. "What do you want me to do?" she whispered.

He nodded toward his left. "Stay here while I search the apartment."

Jessica started to protest but thought better of it. She was no longer a police officer, and she needed to let Ryan take the lead in this situation.

Within minutes, he was back. He stopped beside her and holstered his gun. "There's nobody here."

She breathed a sigh of relief and slipped her gun back into its holster. Then she directed her gaze to the body of the young man lying on the floor.

She'd never liked this part of being a police officer, arriving at a murder scene and looking down at the victim for the first time. During the years she was on the force, she'd had to work hard not to let her fellow officers know just how badly a death scene affected her. And this one was no different.

The air in the apartment seemed to suddenly grow hot, and her stomach roiled at the lingering smells of cooked food and stale cigarettes. Bile rose in her throat, but she swallowed it back as she pulled a pair of latex gloves from her jacket pocket and put them on. Now for the second-hardest thing. She squatted beside the body and felt for a pulse in the neck. No heartbeat, as she'd suspected. Sadness welled up in her at the memory of Richard behind the counter at the store the day before. Had he really been involved in the plan to kill Jamie, or was he a victim of circumstances by being there at the same time? Either way, it grieved her to see a young life cut short.

After a moment, she looked up at Ryan and shook her head. "He's dead. You'd better call it in."

Ryan's gaze fastened on her hands. "You still carry latex gloves?"

She nodded. "Yeah, even in the bounty-hunter business, you never know when you're going to have to handle evidence. I try to be prepared."

Jessica pushed to her feet and tried to shake off the nauseous feeling that assaulted her.

Ryan pulled his cell phone from his pocket and punched in 911. After the call was completed, he turned to the superintendent and the young neighbor. "The police are on their way here. They'll want to talk to each of you, so stay around."

The two men nodded and then turned and walked out into the hall, leaving Jessica and Ryan alone with Richard. Jessica turned away from the still body and walked halfway back up the apartment's hallway before she stopped and leaned against the wall. She closed her eyes for a moment and tried to control the shaking that seemed to start at her toes and extend upward through her body.

A moment later, she felt the comforting touch of Ryan's hand on her shoulder. She straightened and turned her head toward him. His dark eyes held a troubled look. "Are you okay, Jessica?"

"I'm fine." She inhaled deeply and nodded. "I suppose it's seeing the body of a young man I spoke with just hours before. It's such a loss when a victim is a young person. I don't understand killers who have such little regard for the gift of life."

"Neither do I," he said as he rubbed her shoulder. "I've missed having you at the crime scenes with me. You always helped me get through the rough part of it."

She laid her hand on top of his on her shoulder. "I think we helped each other." Then, in an effort to divert the conversation before it became too personal, she took a step away from him, but she stopped as a sudden thought popped into her head. "The door was locked when we got here."

"Yes," Ryan said.

She turned and faced him. "Then how did the killer leave?"

Ryan's eyebrows arched, and he nodded. "Good question. Let's check the back door and see if it's locked."

Jessica averted her gaze from Richard's body as they stepped into the living room and through the entrance into a small kitchen. They stopped just inside the door, and she let her gaze drift over the sink piled high with dirty dishes, the counters cluttered with empty tin cans, the floor stacked with garbage. Then her eyes lit on the back door that stood slightly ajar.

Ryan walked over and stood beside her. "It looks like the killer may have made his way out here and then down the fire escape. Don't touch the doorknob because there might be fingerprints here. I wonder if he entered this way, or if Richard let him in at the front door. I'll tell the first officers who arrive to have someone question all the apartment residents to find out if anyone saw anything out of the ordinary today."

Jessica nodded and walked back through the apartment and into the hall where the superintendent and Richard's friend were waiting. Just as she arrived, two police officers appeared at the top of the stairs and headed toward her.

When they reached where she was standing, she pointed at the open door to the apartment. "Detective Spencer is in there waiting to talk to you."

The officers glanced from her to the two men waiting with her. "Don't anybody leave until we talk with you."

The two men nodded, and Jessica leaned against the wall to wait for Ryan. Their visit to Richard Parker's apartment had brought back a lot of memories about working with Ryan. Some were good, but others were troubling. She'd built a new life for herself. She loved being a bounty hunter, but she had to admit, at times she missed the challenges of being a police officer. But she didn't miss crime-scene work. The memory of standing over Richard Parker's body returned and with it the nausea she'd been fighting.

After a moment, she sighed and turned back to enter the apartment. As she walked down the hallway, Ryan came around the corner from the living room. He stopped, and the benign expression on his face gradually tightened into a look of concern. He tilted his head to one side and narrowed his eyes as his gaze drifted over her. "Jessica, are you all right?"

"I—I th-think so," she murmured. But she knew she wasn't.

The memory returned of saluting Richard Parker with her soft-drink bottle the day before, and tears stung her eyes. Now he lay in his living room, the victim of a killer.

The room seemed to have suddenly grown hot, and she struggled to breathe as her pulse quickened. She closed her eyes and brushed her hand across them as a wave of dizziness swept over her.

From far away she could hear Ryan's voice. "Jessica?"

She tried to answer but couldn't. Her stomach rumbled, and for a split second she thought she was going to throw up. Air, that was what she needed.

Without answering Ryan's question, she whirled and lurched from the room. Once in the hallway, she stumbled to the stairs and held on to the banister as she groped her way to the bottom. She'd just stepped into the downstairs entry when she heard Ryan's voice again.

"Jessica! What's the matter?"

The thought of fresh air propelled her to the front door, and she burst into the bright sunshine. A big oak tree, its branches towering upward, stood at the side of the front yard, and she staggered toward it. Reaching out a shaking hand to prop against the tree, she gulped in great breaths of air in an effort to overcome the nausea attacking her.

In the distance she heard a car engine crank and the screech of rubber on pavement as a car accelerated, but she didn't look up. She continued swallowing exaggerated breaths of air.

"Jessica!"

She recognized Ryan's voice, but it was almost drowned out by the increased roar of an approaching car. She started to turn her head toward his direction, but before she could, a force much like a defensive end sacking a quarterback plowed into her from behind.

She hit the ground, facedown, with the weight of Ryan's body on hers as two bullets whizzed over their heads and splintered the bark of the oak tree just inches away from where she'd stood seconds before.

Ryan lay unmoving until he was certain the car had disappeared down the street. Then he jumped to his feet, pulled his cell phone from his pocket and punched in the number for Dispatch. When the operator answered, he spoke quickly.

"Shots fired at officer in front of the Sunny Lane Apartments on Summer Street. Be on the lookout for a late-model gray sedan with two male occupants. Last seen heading west on Summer."

After he'd completed the call, he reached down for Jessica, who was just beginning to sit up. He grasped her hand, pulled her to her feet and wrapped his arms around her. Before he had time to think of his actions, he'd pulled her trembling body closer and rested his chin on top of her head as she burrowed her face into his chest. His hands moved up and down her back, rubbing and caressing in gentle strokes as he whispered soothing words in an effort to calm her.

The front door of the apartment complex burst open, and the two officers who'd been at the murder scene ran out, their guns drawn. "We heard gunfire and then got a bulletin that shots had been fired. Are you two all right?"

Ryan nodded. "We're fine. Just a little shaken up, that's all. The car's long gone, but there's probably a BOLO out by now."

The officer slipped his gun into the holster and returned to the building. "Then there's no need for us to pursue. Patrol will take care of the call. We're waiting for the crime-scene investigators, so we'll be in the apartment if you need us."

"I'll be back inside in a few minutes," Ryan called out as the two officers walked into the building. When the door had closed behind them, he shifted his position, moved his hands to Jessica's shoulders and gently eased her away from him. She stared up at him, a wary expression on her face. He smiled, placed his finger under her chin and tilted her face up toward his. Her unblinking hazel eyes stared up at him. "Are you okay now?"

She swallowed, and the veins in her neck stood out. Her skin had resumed its normal color, and she no longer looked like the pale child she'd resembled when he saw the first signs of her growing panic attack. "I'm fine, but I wouldn't be if it weren't for you. What made you follow me, though?"

He smiled, released his hold on her and took a step back, severing their connection. "Because I knew you were ill."

He didn't blink as he stared into her eyes, and even though she wanted to, she couldn't tear her gaze away from him. "You always could read my expressions."

He chuckled. "Yeah. Your face is transparent. Everything you feel shows up in your expressions." His smile grew wider. "Do you remember the night we were searching for a suspect at that bar in midtown where a rock band was performing?"

She smiled in spite of herself. "Yes. And I found him in a dressing room backstage, and he got the drop on me."

"Then I stopped at the dressing room door and called for you, and you opened the door."

"But you didn't know the guy was behind the door with a gun pointed at me, just waiting for you to come in."

Ryan shook his head. "Oh, yeah, I knew right away. I could read it on your face, the way you kept blinking your eyes and darting glances to the door even though you were telling me that the room was empty and for me to come on in."

By now Jessica was laughing. "And then you shoved the door against the wall with your full weight and knocked the guy to the floor, and I cuffed him." She wiped at the tears of laughter running down her cheeks. "That was one of the best times we ever had. You saved my life that night. It was almost as good as the time we overpowered Rafe Johnson when he was holding a bank full of customers hostage." She suddenly became serious. "You always watched my back. Thank you for doing it today."

"You would have done the same for me, Jessica. That's what we've always done."

She brushed at the debris on her pants, then straightened and took a deep breath. She lowered her eyelashes and after a moment looked back up at him. "I know you don't see my brothers much, but if you should happen to run into them, I'd appreciate it if you wouldn't mention my temporary loss of control here today. They're very protective of me, sometimes too much, and I don't want them to get the idea that I'm losing my edge."

"I would never say anything to them, Jessica. But don't you think it's time you quit trying to prove to yourself that you're as brave and as tough as your brothers? You've been doing that as long as I've known you, and it's unnecessary. You're the smartest and one of the toughest police officers I've ever known. I think you'd take on a raging grizzly bear with a stick and not blink an eye. So what does it matter if you get a little queasy at crime scenes?"

"But I hid it so well that nobody ever knew."

He smiled. "Except me."

"Except you," she said so low that he barely heard the words. "Thank you for not ever telling anybody."

He thought he'd buried his feelings for her deep in his soul, but her words released them from their prison in a warm rush that flowed through him. He wanted to reach out and trail his finger down her cheek like he used to do, but his better judgment warned against it. He inhaled and smiled as he reached up and brushed a leaf out of her hair. "All your secrets are safe with me."

Before she could answer, a van pulled up to the curb and the team from the crime-scene investigation unit climbed out. Mac Barnes's unmarked police car stopped right behind them. He raised a hand in greeting as he strolled around the front of the car, spoke to the investigators who were pulling equipment from their van and headed to where Ryan and Jessica were standing. He stopped beside them.

"Are you the two that got shot at here?" he asked.

Ryan rubbed the back of his neck and nodded. "Yeah, that was us. I saw the car coming and was able to knock Jessica to the ground before we were hit." He pointed to the tree. "The crime-scene folks need to pull some slugs out of that tree and keep them for evidence."

Mac glanced at the apartment building. "Was the victim shot?"

"No. It looked like he was stabbed. Maybe bludgeoned, too. I guess the medical examiner will tell us which."

Mac took a step as if to enter the building and then stopped. "By the way, after you left this morning we got some interesting information about Gerald Price, the guy that was murdered in the riverfront parking lot. He wasn't really a reporter, although he'd been pretending to be one for quite some time. He'd been following both US Senate candidates."

Ryan darted a glance at Jessica. "Why was he following them?"

"He was a private investigator that Cal Harvey's

parents had hired to get to the bottom of their son's death. It seems that the Harveys thought the police and the DA rushed to judgment, and they hired Price to see what he could figure out. Right before Cal and Susan were murdered, Cal had told his father they were working on a story that he said would set Washington back on its ear. They've always thought Cal and Susan were killed because of it."

"So do you think it's possible that Gerald Price got too close to the answer of whether or not the murders were committed by somebody other than gang members?" Jessica asked.

Mac nodded. "That's the way I read it. Of course, we have no idea what the story was about. Gerald Price's car was stolen along with everything in it. We found a parking receipt in his pocket for a hotel in midtown and discovered that's where he'd been staying while he was in town. His clothes and personal belongings were strewn about the room, and it looked like somebody had gone through everything. There was nothing about what he'd been working on."

The whole time Mac had been talking, Ryan's mind had been reeling with questions about the night Jamie met Gerald Price. According to Ellie, Jamie had seen the Harveys' names on papers that spilled out of Price's briefcase, but could Price have told Jamie something else? Something that might have put him in danger?

"Mac," Ryan began, "there's something I have to tell you."

For the next few minutes he related the story as Ellie had done for Jessica and him. When he finished,

Mac stroked his chin as if he was trying to digest all that Ryan had said. When he finally spoke, his words weren't what Ryan would have expected.

"If I understand you correctly, Jamie spent some time with Gerald Price a few nights ago, and he encountered Richard Parker yesterday in a convenience store that was being held up by a robber. Now both the men Jamie came in contact with are dead. What are the odds of that being a coincidence?"

Ryan's eyes grew wide. "Surely you don't think Jamie had anything to do with those murders."

Mac shrugged. "I'm not saying that. I'm just saying that something ties him to both these homicide victims, and I'd like to talk to him. Can you bring him to the station in the morning?"

"I—I don't think I can do that." Ryan almost choked on the words.

Mac regarded him soberly. "And why not?"

"Because I don't know where he is. He's gone off somewhere, but he wouldn't tell me where."

"This isn't good, Ryan," Mac said as he shook his head slowly. "You've been on the force long enough to know that this will send up red flags back at headquarters. Jamie has ties to two homicide cases, which automatically targets him as a person of interest. But the fact that he's disappeared makes it look even worse for him."

"I know," Ryan muttered.

"You need to find him."

Ryan nodded. "I will, Mac. And I'll bring him in."

"You have any idea how you're gonna go about it?"

Ryan shook his head. "No. The only thing I can

think of is to ask the chief for some time off so I can concentrate on finding him."

"And I'll help him."

Ryan jerked his head around to stare at Jessica. "Are you sure you still want to do that? Especially after…well, you know, after what happened earlier."

She nodded. "We'll find him, Ryan." She turned to Mac. "Don't worry. I know you don't think Jamie had anything to do with these murders, but he may have some information that will help find the guilty person. As soon as we locate him, we'll bring him straight to the station."

Mac glanced from Ryan to Jessica and then nodded. "Okay, but keep me informed. I want to know what's going on." He exhaled and straightened his shoulders. "Now I need to get to work. I'll go on up and take a look around at this murder scene. Want to come with me, Ryan?"

"I've already talked with the guys that are there. I think Jessica and I will get out of here, if that's okay with you. We need to decide what our next move will be."

"Then I'll see you later."

Mac didn't look back as he strode to the door. When he'd entered the building, Ryan turned to Jessica. "Are you sure about this? I thought you might change your mind after what happened in the apartment."

She spread her hands in dismay and frowned. "I really don't know what happened. I think it was all the smells in that closed-up apartment combined with the scent of death that made me ill for a few minutes, but I'm fine now. And I want to help you find Jamie. So why don't you take me back to the precinct so I can pick up my car. We can talk on the way about what our next move is going to be."

She didn't wait for him to answer but started walking toward his car, which was parked at the curb. Her back was straight and her auburn hair sparkled in the sun. He glanced down at his hands and remembered how he had rubbed her back to comfort her, and his skin warmed. It had seemed so natural to hold her close while she regained her composure, and she didn't seem to resent his arms around her. Maybe that was a good sign that she had begun to forgive him for the past.

The warm feeling vanished as quickly as it had come as his gaze fell on the tree and the splintered bark where the bullets had struck. He replayed the events of the shooting in his mind from the time he stepped out the door until they were flat on the ground.

Jessica had come outside first, and he had just pushed the front door open when he saw the gray sedan barreling down the street. It seemed reasonable to assume the shooter was after Jessica not him.

A chill ran up his spine at the chain of events that had taken place since Jamie went to cover the senate candidates' debate. A private investigator he'd met there had been murdered, a convenience-store clerk had possibly been in on an attempt on Jamie's life and had been murdered afterward, and now Jessica, who'd been responsible for foiling the robbery, had almost been killed in a drive-by.

Coincidences? He didn't think so. Their one common denominator was Jamie.

"Oh, Jamie," Ryan muttered to himself. "Where are you and what have you gotten involved in?"

SIX

When Jessica had told Ryan the night before that they needed to decide what their next move would be, she had no idea it would involve a trip to Nashville. But here they were, speeding down Interstate 40 on their way from Memphis to Nashville. And they weren't bound there in hopes of catching a glimpse of a country-music star. They were on their way to the state prison.

They had been very quiet ever since leaving Memphis, and she had enjoyed the time just looking out the window and watching the landscape change as they traveled across the state. The flatlands of West Tennessee, home to some of Tennessee's best farmland, had given way to the hills of middle Tennessee and its rolling hills and valleys with rippling streams.

She gazed out the window at the Harpeth River as they sped across the bridge that spanned the major tributary to the Cumberland River. The sun sparkled on the water that rippled along on its journey, and she sighed in contentment.

"In the beginning, God created the heavens and the earth."

Ryan glanced at her. "What did you say?"

Jessica's face grew warm. "I didn't realize I'd spoken. I've been enjoying the scenery, and the verse about creation came to mind. I suppose it was a prayer of thanks that I breathed out loud."

He smiled and directed his gaze back to the highway. "Your deep faith in God was always one of the things I admired most about you."

Her eyes grew wide. "That's a shock. You never would listen to me when I tried to tell you what trusting God had meant in my life. And if I ever invited you to go to church or to a Bible study with me, you always had an excuse."

"I know, and I'm sorry about that." He glanced at her. "But I was listening, Jessica. After you transferred out and wouldn't talk to me, I was so miserable trying to cope with my job and with Jamie that I decided to see what all that faith stuff was about."

"What did you do?"

"To tell you the truth, I didn't know where to start. I wanted to ask you, but you weren't around anymore. So I asked the precinct chaplain. He told me about a Bible-study group he thought I might enjoy. It was taught by a young preacher at a church near where I lived. I went one night, and I felt at home from the beginning. The group was made up of people like me, men and women searching for something to give their lives meaning. After two months in the group, I turned my life over to God, and I've never been happier or more at peace."

Jessica reached over and squeezed his arm. "I'm so happy for you, Ryan. Do you attend church anywhere?"

He nodded. "Yeah. I go to Grace Community Church, the same place where I started with the Bible-study group. And I mentor some of the high school guys there."

She could hardly believe what he was saying. "Why didn't you tell me this earlier?"

He shrugged. "I don't know. It just didn't come up, but I wanted you to know." He paused a moment and took a deep breath. "If it wasn't for you, Jessica, I never would have gone to that Bible study. I kept thinking about all the things you'd said to me about how God had taken care of you, and I wanted that in my life."

Tears welled up in her eyes, and she turned her head to stare out the window. "So even though you thought I was unreasonable and behaving contrary to how a Christian should act, you wanted what I had in my life."

He exhaled a deep breath. "One of the first things I learned from reading the Bible was that nobody is perfect. We all make mistakes, but if God can forgive us for those things then we should forgive each other also. I've prayed ever since that one day you would forgive me for the mistakes I made. I hope you have."

The past few days had brought many unexpected things into her life, but none had been more startling than Ryan's revelation that he was a believer. And he appeared to have a deeper understanding of what forgiveness was all about than she did. That thought made her cringe with shame. Ryan had laid his heart out in trying to make amends for past mistakes, and now it was her turn.

She looked back at him and could see the muscle

in his jaw flexing as if he dreaded hearing what her reply would be. "Ryan, I'm so happy for you. And I'm also sorry for the way I've acted toward you for the past few years. Please forgive me. I haven't been fair to you, and I sure haven't done what God would have me do. I hope we can start with a clean slate and be friends. I've missed you."

He turned his head and stared at her for a moment before he swallowed. His Adam's apple bobbed, and his eyes held a sad look. "I've missed you, too, Jessica. I can't tell you how happy I am to have you with me on this hunt for my brother."

"And it means a lot to me that you would want me here." She couldn't stop the smile she gave him.

But not a moment later, her expression sobered as she thought about their destination. "What is the plan once we get to the prison?"

He shifted in his seat and directed his attention back to the highway in front of them. But Jessica thought there was a new lift to his shoulders, and the tenseness she'd detected in his body was gone. "Since Tommie Oakes is the one doing time in the state prison for killing Cal and Susan Harvey, I thought we needed to talk to him. Maybe he has some information about Lee Tucker and why his DNA would have been found at the crime scene."

"Was it difficult to get us approved for a visit?"

Ryan shook his head. "Not really. I called the visitation staff yesterday afternoon and explained our link to the conviction of Oakes, and they approved it. We won't have a private meeting with him, but we can talk with him in the visitation gallery along with other inmates who have visitors. Even though we've been put on the approved list of visitors for today, we have to check in and go through security just like everyone else entering the facility."

"I've been to several other prisons before, looking for leads to a fugitive, but never this one. What do we have to do?"

"First off, I assume you have your gun, because I'm wearing mine. They know we're licensed to carry, but we can't take them inside. So we have to store them securely in the car before we go inside. Then we report to the checkpoint area. There we'll be searched with a metal detector and then we'll show the guards our official IDs. They should have the written authorization for us from the warden. After we've completed all that, they'll give us an identification tag, stamp our hands with ultraviolet ink and admit us to the visitation gallery."

Jessica nodded. "That sounds about like what I expected. So, how much longer do you think it will be before we get there?"

"Maybe forty-five minutes."

She reached for the volume dial of the radio. "Then how about some music on our way into Music City?"

A country-music station blared out as she adjusted the sound, and she settled back to listen. Before the next song could play, however, a deep, masculine voice filled the car as a campaign ad for Senator Mitchum began to play.

Jessica and Ryan exchanged glances as the narrator listed all the accomplishments Senator Mitchum had made during his years in the Senate. His war on drugs, his efforts for the military and veterans in his role on the Armed Services Committee and his dedication to the people of the state where he'd lived all his life. The ad finished with a caution to voters not to be swayed by the heroic actions of his opponent, who had no experience in elected office, but to support the man who had led the fight for Tennessee citizens and their jobs for years.

Ryan glanced at Jessica when the campaign spot ended and the music began to play again. "Did that convince you to vote for Senator Mitchum?"

She shook her head. "Still undecided. But with the election not far away, I'm going to have to decide soon. In the meantime, I think I'll take a short nap the rest of the way to the prison."

With a yawn, she settled back in her seat and closed her eyes. She hadn't slept well last night after the drive-by shooting, and she felt tired. As she thought about all that Ryan had said and mulled over every word in her mind, she began to grow drowsy. The next thing she knew, Ryan was shaking her shoulder.

"Jessica, wake up. We're here."

Startled, she sat up and peered out the window. They were parked in a lot outside the facility that housed some of the most hardened criminals in the state. Although the prison was new and state-of-the-art, she still wouldn't have felt comfortable entering alone. But she didn't have to. Ryan was with her, and she felt good about that.

She reached up and pulled down the sun visor with the lit mirror on the back. "Let me check my makeup before we go in."

Ryan burst out laughing. "Jessica, we're not here to impress anybody. All we want is information."

She arched an eyebrow at him, and he looped his arm

across the steering wheel and grinned broadly. "You could be on the pursuit of the FBI's number one most wanted, and you'd have to make sure your makeup was okay. I'm glad to see you haven't changed."

She swatted his arm and couldn't help but grin at his teasing. "A girl likes to look her best no matter what she's facing. I'm sorry if you disapprove."

He shook his head and his eyes softened. "I don't disapprove. From where I sit, you look perfect no matter what. But then, I always thought that about you."

Her ears burned, and she directed her gaze to the mirror. His words had set her heart racing, and she didn't dare let him see the effect he'd had on her. After a moment, she flipped the sun visor to its regular position and reached for the door handle.

"Now all I have to do is lock my gun in the trunk, and you won't be able to tell me from anybody else visiting today."

She'd just finished speaking when a taxi pulled to a stop at the entrance. A young woman climbed from the backseat of the cab. She held a baby in one arm and pulled a little boy who looked to be about four or five years old with the other hand. She propped the baby against her hip so that its head rested on her shoulder and grabbed for the boy, who was struggling to pull free.

"Joey," she yelled, "hold my hand!"

The child pulled against her. "I want to go see Daddy," the child screamed.

The mother jerked him toward her with such force that he plowed into her body. She grabbed his chin and held him still while she glowered down at him. "I'll take you to see your daddy. And if you don't behave, I'll tell one of the guards to lock you up in a cell, too. With the way you act, it won't be too many years before you'll be right here with him."

With that, she strode toward the entrance, the baby's head bouncing against her shoulder and the crying boy being dragged behind her.

Jessica watched them go and fought the tears that filled her eyes. When she turned to Ryan, she could tell he'd been as upset by the scene as she was. She bit down on her lip. "That was very sad to see."

He turned to her, and she was struck by the look of despair in his eyes. "It was. Several of the boys I mentor at church have fathers in prison, and I know what they're going through. That child is on the same path as they are. I feel so helpless that I can't do more for them."

"You're there for them, Ryan. That's the important thing, and I'm sure they know that."

"I hope so." He took a deep breath. "Now, let's get our guns stored so we can go in."

They walked to the back of the car, and Ryan raised the trunk lid. Minutes later, the guns were secured in a lockbox, and they were walking toward the entrance. Other people had arrived and milled forward to enter.

Jessica looked around at what appeared to be family members, young women with children, teenagers with graying grandparents, a priest and a few other men who carried Bibles. All bound for the same destination, a visit with an inmate.

Were any of them here on a mission the way she and Ryan were today? And could Tommie Oakes shed any light on why Lee Tucker's DNA was found at Cal and Susan Harvey's murder scene?

All she could do was pray that he might have some useful information that would lead them to the answer to Jamie's connection to the case and his present whereabouts. And from the look on Ryan's face, that was exactly what he was praying also.

Ryan sat patiently beside Jessica where the guard had positioned them in the visitation gallery and watched the area fill up. The guard had tried to place them in a somewhat private area of the room, but he had cautioned them that he might have to change their seating if the room became too crowded with other arriving guests. So far it looked as if they would be all right, but there were a lot of groups waiting for the arrival of their inmate, just as he and Jessica were for Tommie Oakes.

Jessica hadn't said anything since entering the gallery. She had sat quietly and stared at the gathering crowd. He leaned over and whispered to her, "Are you all right?"

She turned a dazzling smile on him and tilted her head to one side. "Don't worry, Spencer. I'm back in cop mode. I don't plan a repeat of yesterday's little fiasco."

"It wasn't a fiasco," he replied. "It could have happened to anybody."

"Yeah, but it didn't. It happened to me, a bounty hunter with the Knight Agency. If word gets around about my weak moment, it might cost us some business."

He raised his hand and smiled. "I promise to never

breathe a word about it. As I told you, your secret is safe with me."

She laughed and started to reply but stopped when the door opened and Tommie Oakes walked into the room. "He's here," she whispered.

Ryan turned his head to look in the direction she was staring and saw Tommie Oakes for the first time since his trial four years before. He still looked the same. His dark skin was marked with tattoos—some gang symbols and some that probably had other meanings to him—and he still wore his hair long with plaits hanging down around his head. He was dressed in the official blue uniform of the Tennessee Department of Corrections, according to guidelines—the shirt not opened past the second button from the collar of the tucked-in shirt, no sweatshirt underneath and no jewelry.

Ryan remembered seeing Oakes brought in when he was first arrested and the gold chains and rings he'd had on then. Those, along with his gang bandana, were long gone.

As Tommie looked over the crowd, his gaze came to a stop on Ryan, and Tommie's mouth curled into a sneer. He hesitated for a moment before the guard urged him forward. He took a reluctant step and then another until he stood facing Ryan.

Ryan started to reach out to shake his hand and then thought better of it. They'd been warned there was to be no touching between inmates and visitors. He took a deep breath. "Hello, Tommie. Remember me? I'm Detective Ryan Spencer. I worked your case when you were sent here, and this is my friend Jessica Knight."

He glared at Ryan a moment before he glanced at Jessica. "You a cop, too?"

"No," she said. "I used to be, but I'm a bounty hunter now. And I'm looking for a fugitive I thought you might have some information about."

Tommie snorted in disgust. "I don't know nothin' but what goes on in my cell block. And far as I know, we ain't had nobody bust out of there."

She smiled and pointed to the seat across from her. "I know that. But you may know this person. He seems to have a link to you. Won't you sit down and let us talk to you?"

He glanced from her to Ryan and then around the room before he sighed and sat down. "Might as well. Don't look like my old lady's gonna show today for visitation. Course, she don't come much anymore. From what I hear, she done found another guy to take my place. That's what happens when you find yourself behind bars."

"I'm sorry to hear that, Tommie," Ryan said. "Or would you rather we call you Cruiser? I know that was what you went by before you came in here."

"That was what my brothers called me, but not many of them around here. So you can call me Tommie. That's my name. Now tell me what you two doing here and what you think I might help you with."

Ryan cleared his throat and sat up straight. "Have you ever heard of a man named Lee Tucker?"

Tommie's mouth dropped open and his eyes grew wide. "What you want to know about him?"

"Only if you know him or not."

Tommie shook his head slowly. "I ain't never heard of him until last visiting day—last Saturday it was."

Ryan frowned. "How did you hear about him then?"

"This young kid visited me and asked me if I had ever heard of a man named Lee Tucker. I told him no and asked him why. He said might be that this Tucker guy had something to do with killin' those two reporters I done got sentenced to life for. I asked him what made him think that, and he just kinda smiled to himself and said he had some kind of lead that might help me prove I didn't kill them folks."

Ryan's hands started to shake, and he clutched them together in front of him. "Who was this kid?"

Tommie shrugged. "Some college kid from Memphis. Said he worked on a school newspaper. I laughed at him and asked him what made him think that. He said he didn't want to tell me more right then, but he'd be in touch and if I believed in prayer, I'd better start praying he could find this guy."

Although Ryan knew before he asked, he had to know for sure. "Do you remember what this kid's name was?"

"Yeah. Jamie something. It started with an *S*, I think." He frowned and appeared to be concentrating when suddenly his eyes grew wide, and he gasped. "Spencer! That's what he said. Jamie Spencer. He related to you?"

Ryan almost bent double from the pain that felt as if he'd just been punched in the stomach. "Yeah. He's my brother."

"Your brother? Then what's all this stuff he talkin' about? Who this Lee Tucker, and what's he got to do with me?"

Ryan shook his head slowly. "I don't know. His name has come up in another investigation, and it looks like there may be some evidence to link him to the Harvey killings. Are you sure you don't know him?"

Tommie thought for another moment before he answered. "I ain't never heard that name, but I may know somebody can help you. Go down on Beale Street in Memphis and ask around about Kenny Macey. If this Tucker fellow is active in Memphis, Kenny will have heard of him. He keeps his ear to the ground."

"I'll do that. Where will I find this Macey?"

"Don't know. You just gotta look for him. You'll know him when you see him 'cause of his eyeglass."

Ryan frowned. "There's something different about his glasses?"

"Naw, man. It's his glass. Just look for him. He'll be dressed real crazy-like."

"Okay, but there are a lot of crazy characters down on Beale Street."

"You got that right." Tommie frowned and tilted his head to one side. "Is your brother one of 'em? I ain't never heard of him until he showed up here. Got me all excited thinking he might know something that could get me out of here. But you don't seem to think so."

Ryan spread his hands in a gesture of uncertainty. "I have no idea, but I wouldn't recommend pinning your hopes on anything Jamie said. The police will let you know if there's anything new related to your case."

Tommie shrugged and exhaled. "Well, I ain't going anywhere, that's for sure. If you find out anything, I'd like to know."

Ryan pushed to his feet. "We'll do that. Thank you for seeing us today. And take care of yourself in here."

A sad smile pulled at Tommie's mouth. "I do that all the time. I got friends, and we watch each other's backs. Sometimes it don't help, though, and I think about giving up." His eyes hardened, and he glared at Ryan. "But I ain't guilty of killing those folks in Memphis. I got a son and I want him to know it, too. So I keep hoping."

"Then don't give up, Tommie," Jessica said.

Tommie looked at the two of them, gave a nod and walked back to where the guard was standing. He went out the door without looking back.

Ryan took Jessica by the arm and they made their way back to the checkpoint to return their visitor badges and exit the facility. When they were in the car again, Ryan turned to her. "What did you think?"

"I think we need to find Kenny Macey and see if he's ever heard of Lee Tucker."

"I think you're right," Ryan said as he started the car and pulled into the Saturday afternoon traffic.

Within minutes they were back on Interstate 40 headed west to Memphis. As they discussed the visit to the prison, Ryan was struck by the easy way in which they were able to talk, not at all the way it had been just a few days before when he'd encountered Jessica at the convenience store. Even though he was worried about Jamie and irritated at him for getting himself involved in something that needed to be left to the police, he couldn't help but be thankful that his brother's actions had been the catalyst that brought about his renewed friendship with Jessica.

He'd wanted that for so long, and at last it seemed to be what she wanted, too.

He tried to shake thoughts of Jessica from his mind and concentrate on the traffic. Interstate 40 was the third-longest in the nation and the major east–west highway for truckers traveling from anywhere between Wilmington, North Carolina, and Barstow, California. Drivers along it had to be wary of the heavy transport trucks that traveled the route.

And today was no exception. One after another, 18-wheelers passed them on their way west, and Ryan kept an eye on the speedometer to make sure he wouldn't become the next one pulled over by a Highway Patrolman trying to keep travelers safe.

Another large truck passed, and his car vibrated from the rush of wind generated by the vehicle. He slowed a bit and caught sight of the entrance of a bridge across one of the rivers along the route.

As the car approached the midpoint of the bridge, Jessica, who for the past few minutes had been staring in the side mirror mounted outside her window, sat up straight and frowned. "That SUV behind us is getting a bit too close." She leaned forward and narrowed her eyes. "Oh, he's going to pass us."

Ryan glanced to the left as the SUV, in a burst of speed, pulled even with them. Then he gaped in horror as the vehicle swerved toward them, knocking them against the passenger side of the bridge. Jessica screamed at the sight of sparks flying along the railing where the car sideswiped the surface.

The SUV veered away from their car, and Ryan wrestled with the steering wheel as he tried to guide the car back into the middle of their lane. But suddenly the SUV swerved back toward them and knocked them against the railing once more.

The railing shattered, and with a sickening thud the front end of their car crashed through the barrier. One hundred feet below, the river raged. Ryan only had time to offer a quick prayer and grab Jessica's arm before he closed his eyes and waited for them to nose-dive into the murky waters.

SEVEN

Jessica felt Ryan grab her arm, and she braced herself for the drop to the river below. The front of the car tilted forward, and then it bobbed to a stop in midair as if it were suspended on a giant crane. Her head jerked forward and then slammed back against the seat, her breath shattering in her chest.

She shook her head in an effort to clear the blood pounding in her ears and took a deep breath as she stared through the windshield at nothing but a white void and the sky above. A muffled scream rose in her throat at the reality of their situation. They had crashed through the barrier and were now teetering on the edge of the bridge toward the river below.

Ryan's hand on her arm tightened, and she twisted in her seat to get a better look at him. The front of the car dipped forward and then stopped as if balanced on an invisible platform.

"Don't move." Ryan spoke calmly, although she heard fear in his voice. "The back of the car must be caught on something that's keeping us suspended in the air. The slightest movement could cause us to crash to the water."

Jessica started to nod but thought better of even that slight movement. She closed her eyes for a moment and took a deep breath. "What do we need to do?"

"Keep still until help arrives. Don't worry. I'm sure we'll be out of here in no time at all."

She was still facing him as she opened her eyes and saw the look of concern that flashed across his face. A nervous smile pulled at her lips. "You don't have to put up a good front for me. I understand what a precarious position we're in right now. We're going to go over the side any minute. I know what will happen when we hit the water below. If I don't make it and you do, tell my family I love them."

He still had his hand on her arm, and he squeezed it tighter. "Don't talk like that. We're going to make it out of here."

"I don't think—"

Before she could finish her sentence, a voice rang out from behind the car. "Are you all right in there?"

Ryan stiffened, but he didn't let go of her arm. "We're fine for the moment. Who are you?"

"My name is Pete Harper. I'm a truck driver, and I saw that SUV force you into the side of the bridge. I've called 911, and they're sending emergency crews. They should be here soon."

"Good!" Ryan yelled. "Is there anything we can do?"

"Just sit still and—"

A sudden screech split the air and the car dipped forward. Jessica screamed and braced her feet against the floorboard. "What happened?"

"The car slipped forward a little," Pete yelled back.

"Don't move. One of my trucker buddies just stopped. We're gonna try something."

Jessica closed her eyes and thought of her parents and her brothers. How would they react when they heard of her death? Especially her dad. As the only girl, she'd been the apple of her father's eye since she was little, and he had been the most outspoken about her decision to enter police work and then to join the family's bounty-hunter business. He'd always wanted her to have a safe profession like her mother, who was a nurse. But that hadn't been Jessica's choice. Would he blame himself for allowing her to get into a career he felt was too dangerous for her?

"Ryan, tell my father—"

"Stop it, Jessica," he ordered. "I don't want to hear any of this. We're not dead yet, and if that's what happens, I don't want us to spend our last few minutes together dwelling on sad thoughts. Let's think of something good. Maybe... Why don't you tell me about one of the happiest times you've had in the last year."

She frowned. "The happiest time?"

"Yes. Think of something that made you happy and tell me about it."

She thought for a moment before she smiled. "I guess one of the happiest times was when my brother Adam married my best friend, Claire. She and I have been friends since middle school, and she always seemed like a sister to me. When she and Adam finally worked out all their problems and married, I truly had a sister. The wedding was beautiful, and I've never seen a happier couple."

"Mac told me about the wedding. He was there."

"Yes, he and my parents have been friends since I was a little girl. In fact, I even persuaded him to dance with me at the reception."

"He said you were beautiful that night in your blue bridesmaid dress with a simple bouquet of stargazer lilies. I asked him how your hair was fixed, and he said you wore it loose around your shoulders. That's the way I always liked it."

His words shocked her, but she tried not to move. "I can't believe Mac took such notice that he could describe what I looked like."

Ryan chuckled under his breath. "He noticed because I asked him to tell me how you looked. He said you appeared to be happy, and I was glad."

"I was happy for my brother and Claire."

The memory of Claire telling her she could bring someone with her to the wedding flashed into her mind, and tears pooled in her eyes. She hadn't wanted to bring anyone because in her heart she'd known there would never be anybody who could compare to Ryan.

A tear rolled down her cheek. "Don't cry, Jessica. Everything is going to be all right," Ryan said.

She turned her head slightly so she could get a better view of his face. "No, it's not going to be all right, Ryan, and I need to tell you something while I still have time."

He tilted his head to one side and studied her carefully. "What is it?"

"I'm sorry," she whispered.

He frowned. "For what?"

"For all the time I wasted being angry with you. For not letting you explain your feelings to me. But most of all, for not being there for you when you needed me. I'm to blame for the four wasted years we've spent going our separate ways. Can you ever forgive me?"

A sad smile pulled at his mouth, and he stared into her eyes. "There's nothing to forgive, Jessica. I was more to blame than you." He gripped her arm tighter. "But I won't let you give up. No matter what happens I will be here with you. We're still a team. Do you understand?"

"Yes," she whispered. She couldn't pull her gaze away from his face. After a moment, she swallowed and forced herself to speak. "And what about you?"

"What about me?" he asked.

"Tell me something that made you happy this past year."

He was silent for a moment. "I suppose the happiest I've been in a long time was when I walked into that convenience store and saw you. I felt like God had given me a double blessing that day. Not only were you standing in front of me, but you also had saved Jamie's life. I'll always be thankful for both things, Jessica."

Her skin warmed, and she tried to pull her gaze away from him, but it was no use. "As for my saving Jamie, it was really just a matter of being in the right place at the right time."

"You may think that, but I like to think that God put you there to save my brother and to give us a chance to work out our problems."

"Maybe so," she whispered. Neither one of them spoke for a moment but seemed to be lost in their own thoughts. Then a sound at the back of the car caught her attention as the vehicle shook. She stiffened and frowned. "What was that?"

"I don't know." The car vibrated again, and Ryan's fingers dug into her arm. "Pete," he shouted, "what's going on back there?"

"We're trying to stabilize the car," Pete yelled back. "We've hooked a cable to the back of your car and the other end to the front of my friend's truck. He's going to back up until the chain is taut so that your car won't go over. Then we'll see about getting you out."

"That sounds like good news to me," Ryan called. He glanced at Jessica. "Maybe we'll be out of here in a few minutes."

The sound of a revving diesel engine echoed in the car, and she felt the vehicle shudder as the truck backed up. There was a sudden jerk as the car steadied itself, and the front end leveled off.

"Hey in there, can you open the sunroof?" Pete called.

"Yeah," Ryan yelled back as he pushed the button. The sunroof slid back with a swish, and cold air flowed inside.

Jessica looked up through the opening to see a man looking down at her. At first she wondered what he was doing. Then it dawned on her he'd climbed onto the roof of the car and was extending his arm through the opening.

"Ma'am, undo your seat belt and grab my arm. I'll help you through."

Ryan let go of her arm and hit the release on her seat belt before she could reach for it. "Go, Jessica," he urged. "Hurry!"

She gave him one last look before she pushed up

on the seat and grabbed for Pete's hand. Then she was climbing through the opening and onto the roof of the car. Several men standing beside the car reached for her and helped her to the ground, then hurried her away from the wrecked vehicle.

She turned back to the car and pointed. "Ryan," she gasped. "Please help him get out."

The words were no sooner out of her mouth than she saw Ryan climb through the sunroof. It seemed an eternity till he jumped to the ground. He looked at her and took a step, but before he could move, she ran to him and threw her arms around him.

He pulled her close, and she buried her face in his chest as she began to cry. His hand stroked her hair. "Shh," he murmured. "It's all right now. You're safe."

She looked up at him, his face blurry through the tears in her eyes. "I'm sorry to fall to pieces like this, but I'm so glad you're safe," she whispered.

After a moment, he released her and they turned to the trucker who had risked his life to help them. Ryan grabbed his hand and pumped it. "Pete, I assume? How can we ever thank you for saving our lives?"

Pete scratched at the beard that covered his chin and grinned. "Didn't do nothing out of the ordinary," he said. "I'm just glad we had that strong cable. When I first got to you, I figured you'd go over any second. Glad to see I was wrong."

"And so are we," Jessica said.

The sound of sirens interrupted Pete's response, and they looked back down the interstate as a Highway Patrol car, followed by several rescue vehicles and an ambulance, sped along the road's shoulder around the lanes of stopped traffic. Ryan stepped forward to speak to the first officer to climb from his car.

She didn't know what was said, but within minutes she found herself on a gurney being rolled toward the open back door of an ambulance. She pushed up on her elbows and frowned at the young EMT who hovered over her. "Where are you taking me?"

"Your friend thinks you need to be checked out at the hospital. He'll be joining you as soon as he gets through giving his statement to the police. Now take it easy, and everything will be fine."

"But there's no need for me to go to the hospital," she argued.

The young man smiled. "It's standard procedure, ma'am. The police have requested it, and we just want to make sure you're all right."

"Ryan!" she called out, but it was too late. The ambulance door slammed shut, and the wail of a siren split the air as the vehicle started to move.

All she could do was lie back and make the best of the situation. Ryan would be at the hospital before long. Then maybe they could call someone to come get them.

As the ambulance roared toward its destination, Jessica lay still and replayed in her mind those moments inside the car when she had thought they would plunge into the river below at any minute. Ryan had done everything he could think of to keep her mind off what was going to happen, even to the point of getting her to recall the happiest time she'd spent in the past year.

She tingled with pleasure when she remembered how he had described the way he heard she looked at the wedding. And the way he had stared into her eyes had made her forget everything but the fact that they were together at that moment.

Now as she lay quietly in the back of a speeding ambulance next to an EMT who checked her vitals every few minutes, she realized that something had happened to her during that time she and Ryan had spent together suspended over the river. And a new happy moment had emerged in her life. One that she wouldn't soon forget.

Ryan couldn't wait to get to the hospital. As soon as he'd finished his statement to the Highway Patrol and seen his car loaded onto the flatbed wrecker, he'd been whisked away by one of the officers to the hospital where Jessica had been sent. The officers had insisted he be checked out as well.

Now, after an hour of being poked and prodded and finally given a clean bill of health, he was on his way through the emergency room to the cubicle where she was waiting for him. He spotted the curtained cubicle where he'd been instructed to go, but as he neared it, his steps slowed.

He came to a halt, leaned against the wall and covered his eyes with his hands. His legs shook, too unstable to hold his weight, and he braced himself to keep from sliding down the wall and ending in a heap on the hospital floor. Now that he knew they were both all right, the tension of the bridge incident hit him like an 18-wheeler. He felt as if he was losing it.

There had been many near escapes in the years he'd been working as a police officer, but nothing like today. When the front of the car had first burst through the guardrail on the bridge, he thought it was the end for both Jessica and him. Thankfully, it hadn't been. God had watched out for them today, and he said another prayer of thanks.

After a few minutes, he opened his eyes and straightened. He needed to see how Jessica was making it. The doctor had assured him she had no injuries other than a bump on the head, but he wanted to see for himself. If anything had happened to her... He couldn't even finish the thought.

Now that Jessica had reentered his life, he realized it had been a big mistake not to try to clear up the misunderstanding between them long ago. He was grateful that they'd done so now, that it wasn't too late to regain the closeness they'd once had. But, he told himself, that had happened at a risk to her safety.

With a groan he pounded his fist against the wall. It all came back to his brother, everything he and Jessica had gone through the past couple of days. "Jamie, where are you?"

A nurse coming down the hall stopped beside him, her eyes wide, concern evident in her expression. "Are you all right, sir?"

His face grew warm, and he wondered if his skin had turned red. He nodded. "I'm fine. Just a little upset over the accident I was involved in." He pointed toward the cubicle where Jessica waited. "Is there anyone with Miss Knight, or can I go on in?"

"We're through examining her. You can go in."

"Thank you." He ducked his head and stepped past the nurse. Outside the room he paused and tapped on the wall next to the curtain. "Jessica, it's Ryan. Can I come in?"

"Please do. I've been wondering when you were going to get here."

He pulled the curtain back and stepped into the cubicle. She sat on the exam table with her legs dangling over the side. A bandage stretched across her forehead along her hairline above her right eye.

His feet seemed rooted to the spot, and his pulse raced at how pale she looked with the bandage across her forehead. He willed himself to move, and in two steps he stood facing her. "What happened?" he asked, nodding at the bandage.

She raised her hand and touched it with her index finger. "It's really just a scratch. I must have hit my head against the side of the sunroof when I was climbing out."

Ryan stared at the bandage for a moment before he swallowed and took a deep breath. As hard as it was, he looked her right in the eye. "I'm so sorry for getting you mixed up in this, Jessica. If the car had dropped into the water, we'd probably both be dead now. I can't bear to think you might have been killed because you were trying to help me find Jamie."

She leaned forward and grasped his hand. "None of this is your fault. We chose dangerous professions, and we have to accept the risks that go with them."

"No!" he growled and jerked his hand away from her. "You don't have to take the risk for something my immature brother got mixed up in. I think it would be better if we stop this search together right now. I'll go it alone. If I locate Lee Tucker, I'll let you know so you can take him in, but I don't want you in danger again because of me."

Her eyebrows arched. "I don't think you have much

to say about it. I told you I'd help find Jamie, and I intend to do it. You can't dismiss me, especially now. Not when you need me."

"Need you? What makes you think that?"

She hopped down off the table. "Because the last time I saw your car, it didn't look like it could ever be driven again. You don't have a car anymore, but I do."

"Jessica, that's not—"

She held up a hand to stop him. "Save your breath, Spencer. I'm not going anywhere until we've found the answers we need. Somebody has gone to a lot of trouble to keep us from finding out what Jamie has stumbled on, and we can't give up now."

The overhead light reflected off her face, making her eyes sparkle. Even though they'd just come through a narrow escape from death, she almost looked happy. When he had seen her a year ago, she had been angry and hostile toward him. That hostility seemed to have vanished, and he was beginning to see the old Jessica, the one he'd worked with and had fallen in love with. And he liked what he saw.

He smiled. "Okay, if you say so…" He hesitated before he said it. "Partner."

She stuck out her hand. "Partner."

A warm rush flowed through him, but before he could respond, a voice from the doorway interrupted their conversation. "Jessica?"

They both looked up to see Jessica's brother Lucas standing in the doorway. Ryan's first thought was the same as it always was when he saw Lucas. How could he possibly be Jessica's twin brother? They looked nothing alike.

With her auburn hair and hazel eyes, Jessica looked

more like her mother, while Lucas and Adam had both inherited their father's dark complexion. Lucas's dark hair brushed the collar of the leather jacket he wore, and from the stubble on his face, it appeared he hadn't shaved today. A pair of high-priced sunglasses sat propped on top of his head.

He frowned as he let his gaze drift over Ryan before he turned a worried look to his sister. "What's going on? I had a call from the Highway Patrol that you had been in an accident. I got here from Memphis as fast as I could."

Jessica's eyebrows arched, and she glanced down at her wristwatch. "Given the time of our accident and your arrival here, you must have ignored all speed limits."

Lucas stepped over to Jessica and put his hands on her shoulders. "I don't remember. All I could think about was getting here to you. Are you all right?"

"I am." She glanced at Ryan. "Lucas, do you remember Ryan Spencer?"

Lucas glanced at him, and the corner of his lip curled upward. "Yeah, I remember. He's the reason you came to work at the agency with us, isn't he?"

Jessica swatted her brother's arm and frowned. "Don't be rude, Lucas. We've settled that problem between us. Ryan and I are working on a case together, and we had a little accident on the way back from Nashville."

Lucas's eyes grew wide. "Little accident? From what the police said, if it wasn't for some truckers, you wouldn't be alive. Maybe you'd better let this case go. You're not a police officer anymore. You're a bounty hunter."

"And this involves a fugitive I intend to bring in." She reached for her jacket that lay on a chair beside the exam table. "The doctor said I could leave whenever someone came for me. So let's go. Ryan and I can tell you all about it on the way back to Memphis."

Lucas arched an eyebrow and stared at Ryan. "Oh, do you need a ride, too?"

"Of course he needs a ride!" Jessica's shrill voice bounced off the walls. "It was his car that went over the side of that bridge. Now quit acting like an overprotective brother and let's get out of here."

Lucas gave Ryan a wary look and sighed. "Okay, sorry. My car is outside. Let's go."

Ryan didn't say anything but followed the two of them down the hallway and outside to the parking lot where Lucas had left his car. Lucas punched the key fob to unlock the doors, and Jessica climbed into the front seat passenger side. Ryan slid into the backseat and pulled the seat belt tight.

They headed to the interstate, and Lucas turned west toward Memphis. No one had spoken since getting in the car, and Ryan hunkered down, ready to survive a hostile ride back home.

In the front seat, Lucas reached over and tuned the radio to a different station just as a campaign ad for Chip Holder filled the air. Ryan shook his head in disbelief. The media everywhere seemed filled with the election, and if it wasn't an ad for Mitchum, it was one for Holder.

He listened as the narrator extolled the military exploits of Chip Holder as a prisoner of a hostile militant group in the Middle East while he was in the army and how he'd suffered at their hands. The experience, according to the ad, had served as a renewal of patriotism and love for his country and a reminder of the need to support all our military personnel and veterans. The ad ended with a statement that Washington needed new blood with the courage to help overcome the mistakes Senator Mitchum had inflicted on the American people during his tenure.

Lucas turned the radio down as the ad ended and glanced at Jessica. "I like what that guy says. I'm going to vote for him. How about you?"

"I don't know. I haven't decided yet." She glanced over her shoulder at Ryan and smiled, but he turned his head to stare out the window.

After a moment, she settled back in her seat and closed her eyes. Ryan leaned his head against the seat and closed his eyes as they sped along the interstate, but he bolted upright when his cell phone rang. He pulled it from his pocket and stared in surprise at the caller ID. "It's Jamie," he said.

Jessica swiveled in her seat and stared at him over her shoulder. "Answer it and find out what's going on."

He connected the call and pulled the phone to his ear. "Jamie, where are you?" he shouted. "And what are you mixed up in?"

"And hello to you, too, brother," Jamie said. "I just wanted to let you know I'm okay and on my way back to Tennessee."

"Where have you been?"

"I've been in Atlanta, and now I'm headed to East Tennessee to check out some information."

"Jamie, I've been worried to death about you. Why

were you in Atlanta and what lead are you following?"

A long sigh echoed in Ryan's ear. "I'm sorry if I worried you. I should have told you more. I just got off the phone with Ellie, and she said she told you about Gerald Price."

"Yes. And?"

"When I found out he'd been murdered, I decided to go interview Cal Harvey's parents since they had hired him. They were glad to talk to me. They said when Cal and Susan were murdered, they received an anonymous tip about a corrupt public figure who had ties to the military. Since Senator Mitchum was on the Armed Services Committee, they thought it had to be him, and they were investigating his past when they were murdered."

"Did they find anything?"

"Cal's parents didn't know. Cal and his wife were murdered a few days later."

"So they think Senator Mitchum had something to do with Cal's and Susan's murders?"

"Yes, and that's why I'm on my way to East Tennessee and Senator Mitchum's home county. I'm going to nose around and see if I can find out anything from the locals. Then I think I'll take a swing through Holder's home county. But I should be home by tomorrow night."

"Jamie, I don't like this. Come home. Richard Parker, the clerk at the convenience store, was murdered, and the police need to talk to you. I'll go with you to see Mac, and then we can work on this angle together."

"That guy at the store was murdered, too? It looks like this story is getting bigger all the time."

"It is, but you need to get out before you get hurt."

"Don't worry, Ryan. I'll be careful. I promise I'll be home by tomorrow night, and then I'll go to the police with you."

Ryan could hear the determination in Jamie's voice, and he knew it would do no good to argue with him. Maybe he could reason with him when he got home.

"I think you should come now, but I know it's useless to argue with you. Be careful."

"I will. Talk to you later."

The call disconnected, and Ryan glanced up to see Jessica still staring at him. "What did he say?"

He shoved the phone back in his pocket and frowned as he relayed the conversation to her. When he'd finished, she pursed her lips. "So what do we do next?"

Ryan glanced at her brother and noticed how he suddenly tensed at her words. "Jessica, you don't have—"

She darted a glance at her brother and then back to him. "I'm not giving up on this, Ryan. I want to bring Lee Tucker in. Why don't we go down to Beale Street tonight and see if we can find Kenny Macey? Maybe he knows if Lee Tucker has ties to Senator Mitchum."

"Are you sure you feel up to it?" Ryan asked.

Lucas started to open his mouth, but before he could speak, Jessica answered. "I'm fine. Now, what time shall I pick you up?"

Lucas clamped his lips shut, and Ryan couldn't help but grin. He was sure her brothers had learned long ago that once Jessica set her mind to something, there was no changing it. He'd certainly found that out early on in their partnership.

"Seven o'clock be okay?"

"That will be fine."

She turned back to stare out the windshield, and they didn't speak again as they sped toward Memphis.

His thoughts returned to his brother and what he had said about Senator Mitchum. Proving a United States senator was corrupt could be a difficult and dangerous task. He doubted if a college kid who worked on the school newspaper was up to the challenge.

The thought, however, sent shivers up his spine. He didn't want to see his brother hurt. He glanced at Jessica, and his heart lurched at the thought of her being in danger. But it looked as if they were all three headed to a showdown with one of the most powerful politicians in the country. And he didn't like it one bit.

EIGHT

Jessica checked the street number on the mailbox beside the curving driveway that led up to a sprawling house at the top of a small hill. Had her GPS calculated the route to Ryan's house wrong, or had she put in the wrong numbers?

She checked the route she'd programmed in before leaving her apartment. This had to be the right address, but Ryan had said nothing about living in such a lavish house, almost a mansion to her way of thinking. The two-story colonial with its six white columns reminded her of what one might see on a Southern plantation.

Taking a deep breath to calm her suddenly racing heart, she eased down on the accelerator and drove toward the front of the house. She pulled to a stop facing a breezeway that linked the house with another smaller building, probably the garage, but it looked as if it might be large enough to have an apartment above.

The overhead lights in the breezeway burned, and she spotted a door that led into the house. She had just stepped from the car when the door opened, and Ryan stepped out. He smiled as she walked toward him.

"You're right on time," he said. "I just got off the phone with Ellie. I let her know I'd heard from Jamie and that he'll be home tomorrow."

Jessica smiled. "I'm sure she was glad to hear that."

"She was." A smile curled his lips as he stared at her. "Want to come in for a few minutes?"

She came to a stop next to him and shook her head in amazement. "Why didn't you tell me you lived in such luxury? This is a big step up from that small apartment you had when we were working together."

The tip of his ear turned red and an embarrassed smile pulled at his mouth. "I told you my father bought a new house just before he and my mother were killed. I didn't think I could live here at first. It reminded me of my parents. I tried living with Jamie at my old apartment, but he needed a change. We moved in here about the time you transferred to another precinct. It was just what we needed. Both of us realized Mom and Dad had given us one last gift, and we were able to finally come to terms with our new relationship."

Jessica followed Ryan into the house and stopped in surprise. They had entered a sunroom that seemed so inviting she wanted to sit down on the wicker furniture and just gaze out the floor-to-ceiling glass windows. In the backyard copper path lights shed their beams across ornamental grasses that flanked the edges of well-maintained beds of perennials. The sight almost took Jessica's breath away.

"Oh, Ryan," she breathed. "The backyard is gorgeous."

"Do you really like it?" he asked.

"It's perfect," she said. "It's the most beautiful place I've ever seen. You must be so happy here."

He shrugged. "Lonely, you mean. Jamie lives near campus now, and I rattle around in this place all by myself. I'm thinking of selling it."

"Selling?" She whirled on him. "You can't sell this place. It would be a crime to leave that beautiful garden behind. Besides, like you said, this house is a gift from your parents. Keep it. Someday you'll meet the woman you're going to marry, and she'll be thrilled to have such a stunning home."

Ryan stuck his hands in his pockets and rocked back on his heels. "I don't know about that. You never can tell how somebody else is going to like something." He hesitated a moment, then asked her, "How do you like it?"

"I love it. That backyard is wonderful. It sure beats the little excuse for the one that I have." She peered past him. "Can I have a tour of the rest of the house before we go?"

He nodded and motioned toward the door that led into the kitchen. "Come on and I'll show you around. Then I think we'd better get down to Beale Street."

An hour later, as Jessica drove toward downtown, she still couldn't get Ryan's house off her mind. He hadn't mentioned the grandeur of the place since they'd been working together for the past few days, and she wondered why. Maybe he was embarrassed and felt the house was too expensive for a police officer to live in. But from what he'd said, his father's estate had paid for the house, and Ryan's salary, along with money left by his parents, proved adequate for the upkeep. She hoped he wouldn't sell it, but that was his decision. Not hers.

She pulled into a parking lot near Beale Street and found a spot right away. Even though it was still early, the streets were already crowded with laughing and jostling partygoers intent on having a good time. Finding Kenny Macey in this throng might not be as easy as she had at first thought.

"Ready to go?" Ryan asked as he opened the passenger side door.

"I am," she answered and climbed out.

They walked to the middle of the street that the Memphis PD had blocked off so that visitors to the historic district could mingle along the sidewalks and the street between as they roamed the bars, restaurants and entertainment establishments along the famous strip and joined those already having a good time. Ahead she saw a cheering audience clapping and tossing money toward an acrobatic group whose skills seemed to defy gravity.

Ryan and Jessica walked past the performers and strolled on toward the sounds of the blues that wafted from the bars along the street. She kept her attention on the revelers, scanning them as she walked past. She thought of the description of Kenny Macey that Tommie Oakes had given them. "What do you think Tommie meant by 'crazy clothes and an eyeglass'?" she asked Ryan.

Ryan shrugged. "I have no idea. Maybe Macey carries a telescope with him. Just keep your eyes peeled for anybody unusual." He'd just uttered the words when a young woman with purple hair and a nose ring the size of a bangle bracelet walked by. "As if that's going to be hard to do."

Jessica laughed and stared down the street. Her gaze drifted over the crowd in front of her and came to rest on a young man watching two girls singing as they strummed guitars. He wore short pin-striped pants, a waist-link jacket that sported big silver buttons and a safari hat with goggles. But the thing that really set him apart was the monocle that covered his right eye.

"Ryan, it's steampunk," she whispered.

He turned to stare at her, a quizzical look on his face. "Steampunk? What are you talking about?"

She nodded in the direction she'd been staring. "Tommie didn't know what to call it, but Kenny Macey dresses in steampunk clothing. And he doesn't carry a telescope. He wears a monocle."

Ryan's mouth dropped open, and he followed her gaze, his eyes growing wider as he took in the appearance of the man Jessica pointed out. "That must be him. Let's go."

They ambled forward until they were even with the man. Then Ryan strolled around to his left side while Jessica took her place on his right. They waited until the performers had finished their song and the crowd had started to disperse before they spoke.

"Mr. Macey?" Ryan said.

The man turned a startled look to his left. "How do you know my name?"

Ryan pulled out his badge. "Memphis police. I'd like to talk to you a minute."

"I don't have anything to say," he replied and turned to walk away, but Jessica blocked his way.

"Oh, don't be like that, Kenny," she said. "We don't mean you any harm. Just want some information from you."

He glanced from Ryan to Jessica. "I don't talk to cops 'cause I don't have anything they want to know. Now, get out of my way."

Ryan and Jessica both stepped closer until Kenny was trapped like the cream filling of a chocolate cookie sandwich. Jessica smiled. "That's not what your friend Tommie Oakes told us. He said you could help us a lot. Especially with a friend of yours named Lee Tucker."

At the mention of Lee's name, Kenny's face turned white and he glanced over his shoulder. "Don't say that name too loud," he cautioned. "You never can tell who might be listening. Now, get out of my way. I'm leaving."

Ryan laid a restraining hand on Kenny's arm. "Look, Kenny. We don't want to cause you any trouble, but we need some information. Now, we can do this here and be friendly about it, or I can have backup here in minutes, and you'll be in a police car headed downtown for questioning. It's up to you."

Kenny bit down on his lip and glared at Ryan and then Jessica. After a moment, he released his breath and shook his head. "All right. What do you want to know about Lee Tucker?"

"Then you do know him?" Ryan asked.

"I know him, but he's not a friend of mine. He doesn't have any friends. What do you want with him?"

"I'm a bounty hunter," Jessica said, "and he's a fugitive. Skipped bail, and I mean to bring him in."

"And he's also wanted for questioning about a double murder a few years back and the more recent ones of a private investigator down on the riverfront and a convenience-store clerk," Ryan added.

"Wouldn't surprise me any if he was involved with all of them," Kenny said. "Killing is what he's good at."

Jessica's eyes grew large. "What do you mean?"

"I mean he's a hit man. He takes money for killing people. Don't care who they are or what they do as long as he gets paid."

"Does he work alone or does he work for some organization that hires out killers?" Ryan asked.

Kenny shrugged. "I don't know for sure. From what I hear, though, he's been working for the same guy, doing his dirty work, so to speak, for a few years now. But I don't know who his employer is. I heard he was some big politician, but I don't know for sure."

Jessica cast a quick glance at Ryan. "Thank you, Kenny. You've been a big help."

Ryan pulled his card from his pocket and handed it to Kenny. "If you think of anything else you can tell us, give me a call at that number."

Kenny took the card, glanced at it and stuffed it in his pocket. Then he turned and slipped into an alley between two bars. Jessica could hear his footsteps as he hurried away from them, but the darkness swallowed him up. He was lost to sight in seconds.

She sighed and shook her head. "Well, that's another indication that Lee Tucker is working for a politician. But who?"

Ryan rubbed the back of his neck. "I don't know, but the car he was traveling in was registered to Senator Mitchum's campaign. I guess his headquarters is the place to start. Want to go there with me to-morrow?"

"I do. What time shall I pick you up?"

"You don't have to. I called to get a rental car after I got home, and it should be ready for me by the time we get through here. I'm to pick it up from their all-night office on Poplar. Would you mind taking me by there on our way home?"

"I'll be glad to, but do we have to go yet? It's been so long since I've been down here, I'd like to enjoy the atmosphere."

He smiled. "Have you had dinner? We could get something to eat."

"I'd love that. Do you remember the time you brought me to Beale Street to celebrate my birthday?"

His eyes sparkled in the soft lamplight and he nod-ded. "Want to go back to the same restaurant?"

She closed her eyes and licked her lips. "I would love to have some of that crab soup and jambalaya pasta."

"Then let's go." He held out his arm, and she looped hers through it.

Laughing, they walked down the street toward the restaurant where they had once shared an evening that Jessica thought was magical. She didn't know if history was repeating itself, but it felt good to be here with Ryan, to laugh with him and to be free of the negative feelings she'd harbored against him for years. Tonight she didn't want to think about murders or corrupt politicians or even overprotective brothers. She wanted to have a good time with the man that she was just beginning to feel comfortable with again.

Her happy mood hadn't altered a few minutes later when they followed the hostess in the restaurant. They were led to a table near where they had sat the last time they'd been here. Ryan held her chair as she sat down and scooted her closer before he took a seat across from her.

He gazed at her across the flickering candle that sat between them and smiled. "It feels right to be back here with you even if it's not your birthday."

She smiled and glanced up as a waiter arrived and poured them each a glass of water. When he'd walked away, Jessica leaned back in her chair and took a sip from the glass. "Well, you may not remember, but I do have a birthday coming up soon."

He arched an eyebrow and nodded. "Oh, I remember all right. I've never forgotten your birthday."

There was something in the tone of his voice that made her sense he was hiding something from her. She folded her arms on the table and leaned closer. "What aren't you telling me?"

His face flushed, and he picked up his water glass. "Nothing."

She shook her head and narrowed her eyes. "I could always tell when you were hiding something from me. What is it?"

"You're imagining things," he said as he glanced over his shoulder. "Where is that waiter? I'm getting hungry."

She reached across the table and grasped his hand. His eyes widened in surprise as he turned to look at her. "Don't change the subject, Spencer. Tell me what I want to know."

He glanced down at her hand on his, and he swallowed. "I just meant I remember your birthday. Let's just leave it at that."

Jessica frowned and released his hand. She stared at him, but for some reason he couldn't seem to meet her gaze. Suddenly a thought struck her, and she gasped. "You're the one."

He jerked his head up and cast a startled look in her direction. "The one?"

A smile curled her lips, and she shook her head slowly as she crossed her arms and settled back in her chair. "For the past four years I have gotten a notification on my birthday from the children's hospital where I volunteer that an anonymous donor has given money in my honor. I've wondered who it could be, but I never thought of you. But it was you. Wasn't it?"

Ryan's face had turned crimson. He took a deep breath and nodded. "Yes."

Jessica frowned. "But why?"

His gaze raked her face. "On your birthday that first year after we'd gone our separate ways, I kept thinking of when we came to this restaurant. I was so miserable because I missed you so much. I wanted to do something for you, but I knew you wouldn't even open a card from me, much less accept a delivery of flowers. So I decided you would like a donation to the hospital. It didn't matter that you wouldn't know it was from me. I would know and be happy with the fact that maybe I had done one thing you could be happy about."

Tears pricked her eyes. "Oh, Ryan, there were lots of things you did that made me happy, but maybe nothing so much as this special gift. Thank you for honoring me when I wasn't being very lovable, and thank you for giving to the hospital that has a special place in my heart."

Ryan swallowed, and his Adam's apple bobbed. "I did it because *you* have a special place in my heart, Jessica."

She tried to speak, but her throat had constricted. He reached across the table and covered her hand with his. They sat staring into each other's eyes, lost in their own thoughts, and only pulled apart when the waiter arrived to take their order.

The heady feeling of happiness hadn't left her two hours later when she pulled her car to a stop in her parking spot in the rear of her apartment. Ryan, in the rental car they'd picked up on the way back, stopped behind her, turned the engine off and walked around to wait for her to climb from the car.

She stepped out and smiled at him. "You didn't have to follow me home."

He held up a hand to stop her protest and shook his head. "I wanted to. I know you're capable of looking out for yourself, but I had a reason for wanting to see you home."

She placed a hand on her hip and tilted her head to one side. "And what is it?"

His gaze drifted over her face. "I've had such a good time with you tonight, I didn't want it to end. Not many hours ago, we were dangling over a river and expecting to crash any minute. Then tonight we ate dinner in a restaurant that holds some special memories for me. And I want to hold on to every minute I can."

"So do I, Ryan," she said. "Want to walk with me to the door?"

He placed his hand on her elbow and guided her up the walkway to her apartment's back door. They stopped on the porch and she glanced up. "That's strange. The porch light is off. I turned it on before I left. The bulb must have burned out."

"Do you want me to replace it before I leave?"

She shook her head. "No, I'll get the superintendent to do it tomorrow. But thanks anyway." She took a deep breath and pulled her key from her pocket. "I had a wonderful time tonight, Ryan."

"So did I," he murmured. "It's so good to be able to talk with you again and feel like the past has been put behind us." He put his hands on her shoulders and stared into her eyes. "It is behind us, isn't it, Jessica?"

Her heart skipped a beat at the intense look he directed at her. She nodded. "Yes, it's behind us."

Before she thought what she was doing, she leaned forward and pressed her lips to his cheek. She'd meant for it to be a friendly kiss to cement their new friendship, but as soon as she'd done it, she knew that was not what it was at all.

"Jessica." Ryan's hands slipped from her shoulders and he pulled her closer, his lips close to hers in invitation.

She realized the decision was hers. Pull away or yield to what he was offering her. She didn't hesitate, but slipped her arms around his neck and drew his head down. Their lips met, and Jessica's knees weakened. It was as if neither wanted to draw away, but Jessica finally pulled back and stared up at him.

"R-Ryan," she stammered. "I—I don't know…"

He placed his finger on her lips and smiled. "Shh.

Don't say anything right now. This is something we can talk about later." He released his hold on her and took a step back. "Now I think I better get out of here."

She gulped a deep breath to try to calm her racing heart and nodded. "Okay. I'll see you in the morning?"

"I'll be here about nine, and we can go to campaign headquarters. Good night, Jessica."

"Good night."

She watched as he headed to his car and drove away before she unlocked the door and flipped on the kitchen light. Still reeling from the emotions Ryan's kiss had produced in her, she stepped through the doorway to the living room without turning on the light. She'd taken only one step into the room when an arm circled her neck and the barrel of a gun pressed against her head.

Her first thought was the memory of telling Ryan someone could probably break into a bank easier than into her apartment. So much for that assumption.

A warm breath fanned her face as a man spoke into her ear. "Good evening, Miss Knight. A friend told me you want to meet me."

"Wh-who are you?"

His hand released her neck, but the gun pressed harder against her head. She could tell the man was reaching into his pocket, and then he held something up in front of her eyes. Even in the pale light filtering from the kitchen, she knew right away what it was.

"Where did you get Ryan's card?"

The man chuckled. "I took it off Kenny Macey's

body just after he left you and your boyfriend. Now, why don't you tell me why you're so interested in me."

Ryan drove to the end of the apartment complex but stopped in the driveway before he pulled out into the street. He couldn't quit thinking about Jessica and how beautiful she'd looked tonight at the restaurant. It had been a wonderful evening…and then he'd ruined it.

How could he have kissed her? It had taken him four years to even get Jessica to listen to his explanation about what had happened between them. Now that they were resolving their differences, he'd had a momentary lapse in judgment and kissed her. And she had pulled away. Would she ever let him near her again?

How could he face her again if he didn't apologize? He raked his hand through his hair and then propped his elbows on the steering wheel and buried his face in his hands. This couldn't wait until morning. He had to do something tonight.

Before he could talk himself out of what he knew he should do, he'd shifted the car into Reverse and wheeled around to head back to Jessica's apartment. As soon as he pulled to a stop at her walkway, he jumped from the car and strode toward the door, the words of the apology he intended to say racing through his mind.

He jumped over the two steps that led to the small back porch and knocked on the door. When she didn't open the door right away, he banged even louder. "Jessica! I know you're in there. Open up."

He was about to knock again when the door opened,

and she stood before him. He looked past her and noticed that she hadn't turned on any lights other than in the kitchen. She stood there staring at him, one hand resting on the side of the door and the other hanging to her side. "Ryan, what are you doing back here?"

Her voice sounded tight, different. He was afraid he'd blown it with her. But he wouldn't give up without a fight. "We need to talk. Can I come in?"

She hesitated a moment and then blinked. "I don't think that's such a good idea. We can talk in the morning."

He shook his head. "This can't wait until morning. *I* can't wait until morning, that is. I don't want to worry that I've done something to upset you."

She blinked again and darted a sideways glance at the door. "You haven't done anything wrong. It's just that I'm not feeling well, and you need to go."

Ryan narrowed his eyes and studied her face closer. She did look pale, and her hand at her side was clenched in a fist. "What's the matter with you?"

Her eyes shifted toward the door again and he wondered why she kept doing that. Couldn't she even stand to look at him?

She blinked again and sighed. "I don't know. I think it's a repeat of how I felt that night we were at the rock concert."

Her words hit him like a slap in the face. She was trying to tell him something. And he got the message. The memory of that night was still fresh in his mind. He raised his right hand slowly and reached inside his coat for the gun holstered on his belt. "I'm sorry to hear that," he said, keeping his voice even. "I hope you recover quickly like you did then."

"I do, too. I have a feeling I will."

Her eyes locked with his, and he gave an almost imperceptible nod. Then he lunged at the door, throwing all his body weight against it. A loud groan split the air as something—someone—thudded against the wall. He saw a man's hand holding a gun emerge around the side of the door, but Jessica was ready. She grabbed the man's arm with both her hands, raised her knee and brought the man's arm down in a bone-splintering crash across her thigh.

A strangled cry rang out from behind the door, and the gun tumbled to the floor. Ryan scooped it up, pulled the door forward and pointed his gun into the face of Lee Tucker.

Tucker was on the kitchen floor, grasping his injured arm, his face scrunched in pain.

"Jessica," Ryan said, "call 911." He nodded when he saw that she already had her phone out and was speaking with Dispatch.

"They'll be right here," she said as she disconnected the call and turned to Ryan. "Why did you come back?"

His face grew warm, and he shook his head. "It doesn't matter. I'm just glad I did."

"I am, too."

Lee Tucker glared at them. "You won't be after I get through with you. You'll both wish you'd never messed with me."

Ryan shook his head. "Save it, Tucker. You're on your way to jail, and I think you're going to be there for a long time."

Lee shivered and grasped his arm tighter. He turned a look of pure hatred on Jessica. "You're going to pay for breaking my arm. I'll see you dead before this is all over."

Jessica arched an eyebrow as she glared down at him. "Oh, that reminds me. You hinted that you killed Kenny Macey earlier. I suppose we better let the police know that, too. Another murder ought to put you away for a long time."

The wail of a siren split the air, and Ryan glanced out the open back door as a police cruiser entered the parking lot and came to a stop next to his car. The same officers, Jimmy Austin and his partner, who had answered the call to the convenience-store robbery a few days ago, jumped out and ran toward the apartment.

"In here," Ryan called out as they approached the back porch.

Jimmy was the first in the door. In one glance he took in Lee Tucker cringing against the wall and Ryan with a gun trained on him. "What have we got here, Spencer?"

It took only a few minutes for Jessica and Ryan to explain to Jimmy what had occurred there tonight. They told him that Tucker was a fugitive and was a person of interest in a double murder from a few years back, as well as a suspect in the convenience-store robbery and then the murder of Richard Parker. And there was the possibility he was involved in the murder of Kenny Macey.

Jimmy shook his head in disbelief and let out a low whistle. "This guy has been real busy, hasn't he?" He glanced at Lee's injured arm and then to Jessica. "And you did that?"

She nodded. "Yeah. I guess I got a little carried away."

Jimmy chuckled. "He looks like he's in a lot of pain, so I'll leave the cuffs off. I don't want to be accused of administering additional pain to a prisoner." He grabbed Lee by his good arm, pulled him up and propelled him to the door. "Come on. Let's get you down to the station. But first I'll advise you of your rights."

Ryan stood on the back porch and watched as Jimmy and his partner escorted Lee to the squad car. Jimmy finished the Miranda warning just as his partner opened the door and they secured the suspect in the backseat.

When they drove out of the apartment complex, Ryan walked inside. Jessica, busy pouring water into the coffeemaker, glanced up. She smiled and then returned to her task.

"I thought we could do with a cup of coffee." She spooned in the coffee and flipped the switch to begin brewing before she turned around. "Thank you for coming back, Ryan. I—I think he meant to kill me."

Ryan wanted to go to her, to wrap his arms around her and tell her how glad he was that she was safe, but his feet wouldn't move. He simply nodded. "I'm glad I came back, too."

She sank down in a chair at the kitchen table, and he sat down across from her. She clasped her hands in front of her, and after a moment, he reached across and wrapped his fingers around her fists. They were cold to the touch and she shivered a bit. "I was so scared. More than I think I've ever been."

"That's probably the first time anybody wanted to hurt you specifically." He grinned. "Unless, of course, you count being forced off a bridge."

She laughed at that, and the color began to return to her face. "It's been quite a day, hasn't it? We started off at the state prison, nearly died on a bridge and then came face-to-face with an accused murderer who would just as soon kill both of us. I'm glad you finally caught on to what I was trying to tell you about him being behind the door."

Ryan shook his head in dismay. "I'm a little slow on the uptake at times. I kept wondering why you were blinking and glancing toward the door, and then when you mentioned the rock concert, it all fell into place. I'm sorry it took me so long."

"It's okay. You came through when I needed you."

"Don't sell yourself short," he said. "You kept your head and gave me the perfect clue. And you're the one who broke the guy's arm. I'm going to be on my best behavior around you from now on. I don't want to end up the same way as Lee Tucker."

The smile on her face froze, and he realized the double meaning of what he'd just said. Did she think he meant he'd been out of line when he kissed her? Before he could say anything, she jumped to her feet.

"I think the coffee is ready. I'll get us some."

He watched her as she poured the coffee and brought them each a cup to the table. She didn't look at him again but concentrated on sipping the strong brew. He picked up the spoon she'd laid beside him and stirred the coffee.

"I guess this is the end of our partnership."

She looked up, her eyes wide. "What do you mean?"

"Lee Tucker's no longer a fugitive. You've finished your job, and Jamie will be home tomorrow night. So there's no need for us to work together any longer."

"I don't mind helping until you get all the answers about Cal and Susan Harvey's murders."

He shook his head. "That won't be necessary. We're both involved in our jobs, and we have different lives now. I don't see any reason to continue pretending we're partners again."

"If that's what you want." Her lips quivered, and she took another drink from her cup.

For the next few minutes they sat in silence, glancing at each other from time to time. Darting glances here and there and then letting them settle on each other. The silence wasn't awkward, their glances weren't furtive, and Ryan realized he felt comfortable sitting there across from her. He wondered what it would be like to pass evenings like this with someone he cared about. Someone like Jessica.

No, he corrected himself. Not someone *like* her, but Jessica herself.

He remembered how he'd once asked his father how he would know when he found the right woman. His father had smiled and said not to worry about it. He'd know.

The truth was, though, he'd known when he met Jessica that she was the one, but he'd fought against it. At the time, he'd had so many problems in his life he didn't want to involve her in them. Now those problems had resolved themselves, but he thought it was too late for them. Even if she did feel something for him, the time he'd spent with her brother this afternoon let him know her family would never accept him. And he knew from firsthand experience what that was like.

As a child he'd wondered why he never got to visit

his mother's family, why they never sent Christmas presents or birthday cards. It wasn't until he was older that he discovered the truth. His mother's family didn't approve of his father, and they had written her out of their lives when she married him.

His parents had loved each other, but he remembered times when he'd find his mother crying as she looked at a picture of her parents. She'd chosen the man she loved, but it had cost her dearly. He would never put Jessica in the position of having to choose between him or her family. It would be better for her if she found someone her family approved of.

It was time for him to walk away. While he still could. Every minute he spent with her made him want her that much more.

He took a deep breath so that he could try to put in words how he'd enjoyed being with her again, but how it was now time to sever their connection. "Jessica," he said. "It's been—"

Before he could finish the sentence, his cell phone rang, and he pulled it from his pocket. He frowned at Mac's number on the caller ID.

Jessica leaned forward and stared at the phone. "Who is it?"

"It's Mac." He connected the call and pressed the phone to his ear. "Hi, Mac. What's up?"

He listened but couldn't believe what his partner was saying. By the time he had finished, Ryan felt as if he'd been punched in the stomach repeatedly and left to die on the side of the road. "Th-thank you for calling," he managed to say. "I'll talk with you later."

His hands shook so badly that he could hardly disconnect the call. Then he sat there staring at his phone. Rage replaced disbelief and he threw the phone to the floor, closed his eyes and pounded his fists against the table. "No!"

Jessica jumped to her feet and ran around the table to his side. Fear distorted her features, and she grabbed his hands. "Ryan, what's the matter?"

He pushed to his feet and kicked the chair backward. "It's not fair," he yelled.

She grabbed his arms and dug her fingernails into his flesh. "You're scaring me. What's not fair?"

"Jimmy and his partner," he groaned. "They're dead. Their squad car was hijacked on the way to the station, and Lee Tucker has escaped."

NINE

"I can't believe I'm doing this," Jessica fumed for perhaps the fifth time. "Why do I have to go to Lucas's apartment? Why can't I just stay home?"

Ryan's answer was the same as it had been every other time she'd asked the question. "Because Lee Tucker is at large again, and he wants to kill you. You shouldn't be alone tonight. Adam and Claire are still out of town, and Lucas insisted you come to his apartment. And that's where I'm taking you."

She crossed her arms and snorted in disgust. "At least you could have let me drive my own car. I feel like a helpless female who has to be protected by a strong member of the opposite sex, and I don't like it a bit."

"I know you don't, but it's for your own good."

"My own good? My own good?" Her voice rose at least an octave as she repeated the words. "As I've told Lucas and you, I am perfectly capable of taking care of myself."

Ryan gritted his teeth and darted an angry glance at her. "Jessica!" he snarled. "Will you please just give it up? Why can't you put that stubborn streak aside for one time in your life and let the people who care about you help you? Lucas loves you and only wants what's best for you. It's obvious that he doesn't hold me in very high esteem, and I can only imagine what he'd do to me if Lee Tucker came back to finish what he started."

Jessica's eyes grew wide and she stared in surprise at Ryan. "What's the matter with you? I've never heard you raise your voice like that. And I don't like it."

"Well, maybe that's the only way I can get your attention." He raked his hand through his hair and groaned. "When I think how close Lee Tucker came to hurting you today, I can hardly stand it."

Remorse filled her at the stricken look on his face. All Ryan wanted, as did Lucas, was to help her. But she had fought for her independence for so long, it was difficult to give in even when she knew she was in the wrong. After a moment, she sighed and settled back in her seat.

"I'm sorry for being so much trouble, Ryan. I know you're only looking out for my own good. I'll try to do better."

"See that you do." He glanced at her, but the look in his eyes told her she hadn't convinced him she was sincere.

Neither of them spoke for a few minutes, and then she ventured a glance in his direction. "What you said earlier—"

"I said a lot of things earlier," he interrupted. "Which one are you talking about?"

"About our not being partners anymore."

"Oh, yeah. I did say that, and I meant it."

"Well, your argument isn't valid anymore."

He jerked his head around to stare at her. "And why not?"

She batted her eyelashes at him and smiled. "Because Lee Tucker isn't back in custody. I still have a bounty to collect, and I won't do it until he's captured again. I don't think you can argue with that."

"Jessica," he began and then stopped. After a moment, he chuckled. "What am I going to do with you? You always could make me angrier than anybody I've ever known, and then you can charm your way back into my good graces just as fast. You're really a remarkable woman."

"I'm glad you finally noticed."

His shoulders relaxed and a smile pulled at his mouth. "Oh, I've noticed all right."

When he didn't say anything more, she settled back in her seat. "Ryan, are you sorry you kissed me tonight?"

He jerked his head around and stared at her, his mouth gaping open. "What a question for a woman to ask a guy. What are you trying to do, make me feel guilty?"

"No, I just want to know. You came back to my apartment, and I assumed it was because you were sorry and wanted me to know that the kiss didn't mean anything. Just a spur-of-the-moment thing."

They passed a streetlight, and the beam coming through the window lit his face. She could see the muscle in his jaw flexing. "Well, I have to admit I didn't think before I acted. Maybe I should have, but I'm not sorry. I didn't mean to step over the line as far as you're concerned and make you uncomfortable. It's been great having you back in my life these last few days. I'm afraid I took advantage of you."

"You didn't take advantage. In fact, I liked it, too. A lot."

She thought his mouth twitched in a smile, but he didn't look her way. "I'm glad. Maybe we can have a repeat sometime soon."

"Maybe we can. But in the meantime, can I be your partner again? I want to see this case through until the end."

"Oh, all right," Ryan said. "I never could refuse you when you were nice to me."

She sat up straighter. "Good. Now, what are we going to do tomorrow? Go to the candidates' head-quarters?"

He nodded. "I think it's time we spent some time with Senator Mitchum's staff as well as Chip Holder's. Maybe we'll find out something. At the very least, maybe we'll decide who we're going to vote for." He grinned at her. "But you're probably going to vote for Chip Holder. It seems all the women have gone crazy over his good looks and winning personality."

"Don't lump me in with 'all the women.' I decide who I'll vote for based on the candidate's platform not his looks. I'll be interested in seeing what both of them have to say." She leaned forward to peer out the windshield and pointed to the house at the end of the street. "That's where Lucas lives."

Ryan pulled to a stop at the curb, got out and reached into the backseat for Jessica's overnight bag. She waited for him to come around the car, and then they walked up to the house. The front door opened before they reached the porch, and Lucas stepped outside. He walked to the edge of the porch and reached for Jessica's bag as Ryan started up the steps.

"I'll take that. Thanks for bringing my sister over."

Ryan handed him the bag and nodded. "Glad to do it. I didn't think Jessica should be alone tonight."

Lucas grunted. "Glad to see you can be sensible about some things."

Jessica narrowed her eyes and glared at her brother. "There's no need to be rude to Ryan. It's not his fault that Lee Tucker escaped. We're both upset because two officers we know have been killed. You need to be a bit more understanding of what we've been through tonight."

Lucas cast a glance in Ryan's direction and nodded. "Sorry, Spencer. I guess I get a bit overprotective at times. I just don't want to see my sister get hurt."

Jessica threw up her hands in disgust. "What's wrong with you? If you can't be a bit friendlier, I'll get back in the car and have Ryan drive me home."

"No, Jessica," Ryan said. "I understand where Lucas is coming from. He has your best interests in mind. You need to listen to him."

Jessica smiled up at her brother, then looked back at Ryan. "Don't judge him too harshly, Ryan. He really is a good guy once he warms up to somebody. Maybe he will with you before long."

"Maybe so. Now I need to get home. I'll see you in the morning."

"I'll be waiting."

She watched Ryan as he hurried back to his car and then drove away. When she turned to enter the house, Lucas stood near the door, staring at her. "Jessica, what are you doing?"

Her eyebrows arched, and she took a step toward him. "I don't know what you're talking about."

He jerked his head in the direction of Ryan's disappearing taillights. "That guy ripped your heart out a few years ago, and he'll do it again if you're not careful."

She shook her head. "You're wrong, Lucas. Ryan and I are just friends. We're different people now with different lives. There's just friendship between us."

"Tell that to somebody who'll believe you," he scoffed. "I saw how you looked at him on the way back from the hospital today, the same way you looked at him when you walked up on my porch tonight." He put his arm around her shoulders and gave her a quick hug. Then he guided her into his living room. When they sat down on the couch, he took her hand in his and laced his fingers with hers. "All I'm saying is be careful. I don't want to see you get hurt."

Tears came to her eyes and she blinked to keep Lucas from seeing them. "I don't want to get hurt either, but I'm lonely, Lucas. I'm not getting any younger, and I haven't dated anyone since Ryan and I broke up." He put his arm around her and she laid her head on his shoulder. "Don't you ever wish you could find the right person?"

She could feel the beat of his heart as he held her in his arms. "Sometimes I do," he said in a low voice. "Then other times I'm afraid I will find her, if that makes any sense."

"Is that why you change girlfriends so often? You're scared of how your life will change if you do find the right one? Or is it the fact that the woman you loved married somebody else, and you've never gotten over her?"

His face turned a bit red and he shrugged. "Maybe a little of both. But we're talking about you not me. All I'm saying is be careful before you fall in love with Ryan Spencer. He hurt you once, and he can do it again."

"I know," she said. "But there's no need to worry. I think Ryan hinted tonight that he's not interested. At least that's the way it sounded to me." She took a deep breath and sat up straight. "Enough of this. I need to go to bed. Ryan and I are going to talk to the candidates running for the Senate tomorrow and I want to be at my best."

"You're going to see Senator Mitchum and Chip Holder both?"

"Yes, we are."

"I wish I could go with you. I really admire Chip Holder and what he suffered at the hands of that terrorist group when he was held prisoner."

Jessica pushed to her feet. "You're not the only one who feels that way. The polls have him in a slight lead over Senator Mitchum at the moment. I'm looking forward to meeting him."

Later, as she lay in bed, unable to sleep, she thought back over what Kenny Macey had said earlier in the evening. Lee Tucker was rumored to be working for one of the candidates, and word on the street said that his employer was Senator Mitchum. Also, the car used in the convenience-store robbery had been registered to Senator Mitchum's campaign.

All circumstantial evidence, she told herself. But

she'd been a police officer long enough to know that you couldn't ignore any lead. And it certainly looked as if Senator Mitchum might have some explaining to do.

The next morning a little before ten, Ryan, clutching a small bag in his hands, straightened his shoulders and knocked on the door at Lucas's house. He'd had several hours to practice what he was going to say to Lucas about how he'd make sure nothing happened to Jessica. He thought he'd finally bolstered his courage enough to face her brother. At least he hoped he had.

The door opened, and he blinked in surprise when instead of Lucas it was Jessica standing there. Her hair was pulled back in a ponytail this morning, and her face had a fresh scrubbed look that made her eyes sparkle. She smiled and opened the door wider.

"Good morning. Come on in. There's still some coffee left."

Ryan stepped into the living room and glanced around as she closed the door and then stepped up beside him. She looked up at him as if waiting for him to speak, which he realized he hadn't done yet.

He cleared his throat and looked around. "Where's Lucas?"

She laughed and motioned for him to follow her as she walked toward a doorway that led to the kitchen. "He left earlier on his way to Birmingham. He's to pick up a fugitive there today and return him to Memphis. He didn't want to leave me alone, but I knew you'd be here soon."

Despite his earlier resolve, Ryan breathed a sigh of

relief that he wouldn't have to encounter her brother this morning and followed her into the kitchen. "I would have been here sooner but I had some shopping to do before I came."

She had picked up the coffeepot and was in the process of pouring a cup, but she stopped and turned to stare at the bag he'd set on the kitchen table. "What did you buy?"

"Before I tell you, I want you to promise you won't get upset with me. This is just a precaution, but one I think we need to take."

She set the coffeepot down and frowned. "Are you going to tell me or are you going to keep me in suspense?"

He reached into the bag, pulled out two small boxes and set them on the table beside the bag. "I got to thinking last night about all that's happened and how I've been so worried not knowing where Jamie is. Believe me, he's going to get a piece of my mind when he gets home tonight. I can understand Lucas's concern about you, and I thought this might put his mind more at ease."

Jessica rolled her eyes. "Ryan, what are you trying to tell me?"

"I bought us each a personal GPS tracking device this morning. We don't know what Lee Tucker is planning, and I want to take every precaution I can to make sure he doesn't succeed. These little devices are so small—they only weigh about two ounces—and they can be slipped into a boot out of sight. I'll feel a lot better knowing I can keep up with your whereabouts all the time."

She stared at the boxes for a moment before she spoke. "Do you really think this is necessary?"

"I do, especially after what Mac told me this morning."

"What did he say?"

"The police found Kenny Macey's body behind a bar down on Beale Street last night. He'd been stabbed to death."

Her eyes grew wide, and she sucked in her breath. "I was afraid of that." She sat silently staring at the GPS devices for a moment and then reached for one of the boxes and opened it. "How do I activate it?"

"It's already activated, and I've installed the app on my cell phone that will track the device. We can do the same for mine on your cell phone. What do you think?"

He watched her face for the first sign of opposition to the idea, but it didn't come. She pulled the small rectangular device from its box and studied it as she turned it over in her hand. After a few minutes, she looked up at him.

"Is this one ready to go?"

He nodded. "Yes. All you have to do is conceal it on yourself somewhere."

Balancing on one leg, she propped her foot on a kitchen chair, pulled up the bottom of her jeans and slipped the tracker into her boot. Then she pulled the pants leg down, straightened it and lowered her foot to the floor.

"Now let's do yours."

Surprised at how easily she'd accepted his suggestion, he opened the other box. "Give me your cell phone, and I'll get this one set up on it."

Minutes later, with both devices set, they relaxed at the kitchen table and sipped from steaming cups of coffee. He found he couldn't keep his eyes off her this morning and had to fight to keep from glancing at her from time to time.

Finally she chuckled. "What's the matter, Ryan? You're acting like you want to tell me something but you're afraid to say it."

He set his coffee cup down and smiled. "I guess I'm still a little bit surprised at how you accepted the tracker without telling me how you could take care of yourself. I expected a terrible argument when I came in earlier."

She pursed her lips and shrugged. "I did a lot of thinking last night about what you said. You know, about how I shouldn't worry the people who love me. I know Lucas only wants what's best for me, and yesterday's events scared him. It's selfish of me to make my family worry. So I decided I can put aside my independence for a while and try not to upset the people I care about."

"I think that's a good idea." He raised his coffee cup and tipped it toward her before draining it and setting it back in its saucer. "Now, why don't we go see if we can figure out what's going on in the world of politics this morning."

She jumped to her feet, grabbed their cups and set them in the sink. "I'll be right with you. I have to get my gun. I don't feel completely dressed unless I have it."

He watched her leave the room and smiled. The time with Jessica this morning had been good. The all-out war he'd expected over the GPS hadn't come about. Instead, she had been understanding, and her words about not upsetting those who cared for her had touched his heart. She had no idea how right she was. He was beginning to care more every day.

TEN

Jessica stepped out of the car and let her gaze drift over the row of offices that lined the sidewalk along one side of the trendy mall in East Memphis. The sign over one of the doors announced the location as the reelection campaign headquarters for Senator Mitchum. Signs with the senator's picture on it adorned the windows, and a sign on the front door welcomed all to enter.

Ryan glanced at her. "Ready for this?"

She nodded. "Let's go."

Ryan opened the door and they stepped inside to what Jessica could only describe as controlled bedlam. Rows of desks lined each wall and another row ran down the middle of the room. The roar of conversation filled the room as the young men and women who manned the desks were either engaged in telephone conversations or working on computers.

Before they could move beyond the door, a young woman appeared out of nowhere and hovered near Jessica's elbow. She beamed a huge smile that could grace an advertisement for an orthodontist.

"Hello, I'm Cindy. Are you here to volunteer or just to visit with us today?"

Ryan pulled his badge out. "We're here on police business. Is the senator here?"

Her eyes grew large at the sight of the badge and she shook her head. "No, he's speaking at a luncheon at the Peabody today, and he's already left. But his chief of staff is here. Would you like to see him?"

"Yes. Can you show us where he is?"

The girl glanced from one to the other before she led the way across the room where the volunteers worked and through a door at the back. They stepped into a short hallway that had an office on either side and a door at the end with an exit sign over it.

Cindy stopped at the door on the left. "This is Mr. Stark's office. I'll tell him you're here."

At her knock, a voice from inside called out. "Come in."

Cindy stuck her head inside. "Mr. Stark, I'm sorry to disturb you, but there are some police officers here to see you."

"Police officers? To see me? Well, send them in."

As they entered the room, a balding man rose from a chair behind a desk and came across the room to meet them, his hand extended. "Hello. I'm Wendell Stark, Senator Mitchum's chief of staff. Welcome to our reelection headquarters, but I have to admit I'm mystified what the police could possibly want to talk to me about."

Jessica shook the man's hand and inclined her head toward Ryan. "Actually, Detective Spencer is a police officer. My name is Jessica Knight. I'm a bounty hunter."

His eyes grew wide. "Now I'm even more stunned. What brings a bounty hunter to our doors today?"

Ryan stepped forward and shook Wendell's hand and smiled. "We're working on a case together, and we think you may have some information that will help us."

Wendell nodded. "Well, of course I will if I can. What's this about?"

Ryan reached in his pocket and pulled out the copy of Lee Tucker's mug shot he'd gotten at headquarters. "Have you ever seen this man?"

Wendell stared at the picture for a moment before he shook his head slowly. "No, I don't recognize him. Who is he?"

"His name is Lee Tucker," Ryan continued. "He held up a convenience store a few days ago, and the license number on the getaway car was registered to Senator Mitchum's campaign."

Wendell nodded as he handed the picture back to Ryan. "Yes, I knew about the robbery. The police questioned us about the car. I told them it was a car that we had in the parking lot out back. It's driven by one of Senator Mitchum's aides, but he was in Washington at the time with the senator. I suppose that's why we didn't know the car was missing until the police came and told us it had been used in a robbery." He glanced up at Ryan. "I gather the robber hasn't been caught yet, or you wouldn't be here."

"He was captured last night but he escaped. Two officers were killed in the process."

A stricken look lined Wendell's face. "I'm sorry to hear that. I'm sure the senator will want to send condolences to the families. I'll have one of our workers call and get the names of the officers' family members."

"That would be very thoughtful," Jessica said. "One of the officers was a friend to both of us."

Wendell glanced at his watch and frowned. "Is there anything else I can do for you? I've told you I've never seen the man in the picture, and I've explained about the car. I really need to get back to work, unless there's something else I can do. I'm on a deadline for finalizing the senator's speaking tour across the state."

Ryan shook his head. "I guess that's all. We don't want to detain you."

Wendell walked to the door and held it open for them to exit. "I'm sorry I couldn't help you more."

"So are we," Jessica said as she walked into the hallway.

Wendell smiled at them. "Senator Mitchum is a big supporter of the Memphis Police Department. He'll be sorry he missed you. I'll take this opportunity, though, to say that I hope we can count on your vote come election day."

Ryan smiled. "I always vote. That's for sure."

"And so do I," Jessica added.

A slight frown wrinkled Wendell's forehead, but he forced a smile to his face. "That's good to know. If I can be of further service to you, let me know."

"We will."

Ryan took Jessica's elbow and steered her down the hallway and back through the volunteers, who appeared just as busy as they'd been earlier when they entered the building. Once outside, Jessica turned to Ryan.

"What did you think?"

He shrugged. "I don't know. He sounded believable. I just wish we could have talked to the senator." He glanced at his watch. "Let's hurry over to Chip Holder's headquarters and see if he can shed any light on things."

As they walked toward the car, Jessica saw Ryan pull his cell phone out, stare at the screen and frown. "What's the matter?"

"I keep expecting a call from Jamie. He said he'd be home today, but I thought he'd call again to let me know he was on his way. I haven't heard from him since he called yesterday."

"Have you tried calling him?"

"I have, but it goes straight to voice mail. I've left him several messages to call, but he hasn't." Ryan unlocked the car door and turned to face Jessica. "With Lee Tucker at large, I'm really beginning to get worried about Jamie."

Jessica didn't say anything else, but Ryan's words troubled her, too. She couldn't shake the feeling that something wasn't right, and one look at Ryan's face told her he was worried sick. She closed her eyes. *Please, God, keep him safe. He's all Ryan has.*

But her troubled thoughts remained with her all the way to Chip Holder's campaign headquarters.

Ryan was so lost in thought that he followed the car's GPS instructions as if he was on automatic pilot. He turned off the main thoroughfare onto a side street lined with discount stores. At the end of one row of stores, he spotted a sign with Chip Holder's name on it.

Jessica turned to him in surprise. "This is where Holder has his campaign headquarters?"

"Yeah. Quite a step down the ladder from Senator Mitchum's offices, isn't it?"

She nodded in agreement as he pulled the car to a stop in front of the small office. Just as at Senator Mitchum's headquarters, posters for Chip Holder were plastered around the door and in the windows.

They climbed from the car and walked toward the entrance. Ryan pushed the front door open and she stepped inside first. The interior also offered a stark contrast to what they'd seen earlier at the Mitchum headquarters. Here there were only five desks being manned by individuals who looked extremely harried.

As they came to a stop, a young man at the front desk looked up and smiled. His red-streaked eyes and the dark smudges underneath appeared to be effects of lack of sleep. Nevertheless, he jumped to his feet and came around his desk.

"Welcome to Holder campaign headquarters. My name is Mark and I'm a volunteer. What can I do for you?"

Again Ryan pulled out his badge. "I'm with the Memphis police. I'd like to speak to whoever's in charge, maybe Mr. Holder's chief of staff."

Mark smiled. "That would be Mr. Johnson, but he's out sick today. Mr. Holder's here, though. Would you like to see him?"

Jessica's eyebrows arched, and she cast a surprised look at Ryan. "We thought he'd be too busy to talk to us."

Mark shook his head. "Chip's never too busy to talk to a potential voter no matter who they're supporting in the race. He's one of the friendliest guys I've ever met. Come on. I'll show you to his cubicle."

"Cubicle?" Jessica mouthed the word to Ryan as they followed Mark to a small hallway in the back.

Just as Mark had said, several room dividers had been arranged to block off a section of the hallway. The young man paused outside the opening to a cubicle. "Chip, the police are here. They'd like to talk to you."

"Send them in, Mark." The voice Ryan had heard numerous times on television campaign ads boomed out from behind the dividers.

Mark stepped out of the way and Ryan followed Jessica inside. Chip Holder stood behind his desk in the cluttered area, a big smile on his face. In person he looked younger than Ryan knew him to be. He had to be in his early forties, but he could pass for a guy in his late twenties.

His broad chest and bulging muscles in his back and arms were evidence of time spent in the gym, and his blond hair was cut short. He wore a knit shirt much like a golfer would wear, and Ryan suddenly realized in all the pictures he'd ever seen of Holder he had never been dressed in a suit and tie. In all his publicity pictures he either wore casual clothes or his military uniform. Just a regular guy from humble beginnings, he called himself in his ads, a veteran who loved his country and had served proudly.

Holder's gaze drifted over Jessica before he glanced at Ryan and then back to Jessica. He stepped around his desk, his hands outstretched, and took her hand in both of his. His blue eyes twinkled as he gazed down at her. "It's always a pleasure to meet one of Memphis's finest police officers."

The compliment sounded sincere, and Jessica blushed

as if caught off guard. "Actually, I'm not a police officer. I used to be, but now I'm a bounty hunter."

Ryan's skin prickled a little as Holder's eyes grew large. "A bounty hunter? How interesting. I'd like to learn more about your profession sometime."

"I'd be glad to talk with you about it."

Chip smiled once more before he released her hand and turned to Ryan. "And you are...?"

"Ryan Spencer, a detective with the MPD. We'd like to ask you a few questions."

Chip motioned to two chairs in front of his desk and walked back around to take his seat. "Of course I'll do anything I can to help you. What's this about?"

Ryan pulled out the picture of Lee Tucker and handed it to him. "Do you know this man?"

Chip frowned as he stared at it, shook his head and handed it back to Ryan. "No, I can't say that I've ever seen him. That looks like a copy of a mug shot, so I assume he's wanted by the police."

"He is. Among other things, for a convenience-store robbery and for questioning in several murders," Ryan said.

"Not to mention, he's a fugitive from bail on another charge," Jessica added.

Chip nodded. "Sounds like he has quite a criminal history."

"That's what we need to determine. You're sure you've never seen him around your headquarters?"

"No, but there are lots of people who come and go." He stood up. "But if he's ever been here, Mark would remember him. Let me call him."

He went out the door and within a few minutes was back with Mark following behind. Ryan rose as Mark came into the room and stopped beside the desk. "Chip said you'd like to ask me some questions."

Ryan pulled out the picture again and handed it to the young man. "Have you ever seen this guy before?"

Mark stared at the picture for a moment before he nodded. "Yeah, I have."

Chip leaned toward Mark. "He's been here?"

Mark shook his head. "No, I didn't see him here. It was at Senator Mitchum's headquarters last week."

Jessica's mouth gaped open. "What were you doing there?"

"Mr. Stark had called and wanted someone from the staff to come over to their headquarters and discuss the plans for the televised debate. Chip and Mr. Johnson were in Middle Tennessee on a campaign trip. When I called Chip, he asked me to go in his place. I did, and when I walked into Mr. Stark's office, that man was in there. They shook hands, Mr. Stark thanked him for coming and he left."

"Did Mr. Stark introduce you?" Ryan asked.

"No, he just said the man was a campaign worker, and I didn't think anything else about it. We have people coming and going all the time around here."

"Thank you, Mark," Chip said. "You can get back to work, unless Detective Spencer has another question for you."

Ryan shook his head. "No, that's all. Thanks, Mark."

They waited until the young man had left before Ryan turned back to Chip. "We appreciate your time today. But we'll get out of your way for now."

Chip waved his hand in dismissal. "I wish I could have been more help, but maybe Mark's statement helped you some."

"It's certainly given us a lead we'll have to investigate," Jessica said.

Chip walked with them back through the outer office and to the front door. When they stopped there, he stuck his hands in his pockets and frowned. "I'm sure you've followed this campaign, and you know the media frenzy it's created. I'm running for office because I think it's time we had a change in this state. A change from Mitchum with his special-interest groups and his representation in Washington that doesn't amount to more than getting himself a raise every year. Nothing would make me happier than finding proof that he's as crooked as I suspect him to be. He doesn't deserve to represent the good people of this state, and I hope you can find something that will show him up for what he really is."

"One thing I promise you," Ryan said. "We'll follow where the evidence leads. That's all we can do."

Chip smiled. "Then good luck. I hope you're successful." He turned to Jessica and glanced down at her left hand before he spoke. "And I meant what I said about learning more about your job. I'd like to get together with you sometime for dinner. I don't see a wedding or engagement ring, so I hope I'm not out of line."

Her eyes grew wide, and she glanced at Ryan. He tried to control the scowl pulling at his face, but he knew he failed. She turned her attention back to Holder. "N-no. I'm not married. I would love to have dinner with you."

"Do you have a card?"

"Yes." She pulled her business card from her pocket and handed it to him.

He smiled and glanced down at it. "You'll be hearing from me, Miss Knight."

Ryan grabbed the door handle and pushed it open with a shove. When they stepped outside onto the sidewalk, he didn't say a word but stormed to the car and unlocked it. She followed and had barely gotten the door closed before he had the car in Reverse and wheeled around to roar off down the street.

She fumbled with her seat belt and glanced at his profile. "What's wrong?"

He grasped the steering wheel tighter but didn't turn to face her. "Have you decided now who you're going to vote for?"

His heart pricked at the sharp tone of his voice, but it was too late to take the words back. All he could do was try to bluff his way through the emotional toll her actions and words with Chip Holder had taken on him.

She swiveled in her seat to face him. "No, I haven't. Are you all right?"

Despite his intention, he couldn't remain quiet. He couldn't pretend she hadn't hurt him. He pulled into the parking lot of a discount store and threw on the brakes. Then he turned to glare at her. "How could you stand there and let that guy hit on you like that? It was disgusting."

Her mouth gaped open, and she stared at him. "Disgusting? How can you say that? He was being nice."

"Nice? He was flirting with you, and you enjoyed every minute of it. I expected you to swoon any minute."

Her cheeks flamed. "And so what if he was inter-ested in me? Maybe I was interested in him, too."

"He's too old for you, Jessica. And he's a politi-cian. You can't get involved with somebody like him."

The crimson flush of her cheeks had spread to her ears, and her hands gripped her knees as she seemed to try to control her anger. "Then who should I get involved with? You? A man who kisses me and then can't wait to get back to my apartment and apologize."

He leaned forward until their noses almost touched. "And if I hadn't come back, Lee Tucker would have killed you just like he intended."

Tears welled in her eyes. "Well, thanks for remind-ing me how I can't take care of myself. But I think you've just made your position perfectly clear to me. You don't want me. You never did. You've always managed to get rid of me in one way or another. But you're so selfish, you can't let go because you're afraid somebody else will want me. Well, I've got news for you. I'll go out with anybody I want to, and there's nothing you can do about it."

Her words hit him as if someone had thrown ice water on him, and his anger disappeared. What was the matter with him? The last thing he wanted was to argue with her, but maybe it was what he needed after all.

He sighed and rubbed his hands over his eyes. "It's good to know how high an opinion you have of me." He cleared his throat and turned to look out the windshield. "I'm sorry for what I said. I won't inter-fere in your life again. Now, do you want to go home or to Lucas's house?"

"I need to go home. If you remember, you drove

me to Lucas's house last night, and I don't have my car there."

He put the car in gear and without a word drove back into the street. He didn't say anything else until he stopped at the back entrance to her apartment.

She waited a moment, then climbed from the car and walked to her door.

He drove away without looking back.

By the time he'd driven two blocks, he was berating himself for losing his temper and for talking to Jessica the way he had. He pulled over into a curbside parking spot and closed his eyes as he recalled every angry word he'd said.

How could he have behaved so badly and especially with a woman as wonderful as Jessica? She hadn't invited Chip Holder's attention, and even if she had, he didn't have the right to criticize her for accepting it. From what he'd read about the candidate, he had no special woman in his life, and maybe he'd legitimately been attracted to Jessica.

Ryan sure couldn't fault him for that. He was, too. But if he didn't get this argument settled between them, he could kiss any chance he had with her goodbye. And he wouldn't blame her.

Before he realized what he'd decided to do, he made a U-turn and headed back toward Jessica's apartment. When he arrived, he jumped out of the car, raced to the back door and pounded on it. "Jessica! It's Ryan."

No answer.

He knocked again, louder this time. "Jessica, you have to be in there. Open the door."

A muffled cry came from inside. "Go away. I don't want to talk to you."

The sound of her trembling voice made his heart lurch, and he leaned his forehead against the door. "Jessica, I'm sorry. Please let me in. We need to talk."

"I don't want to talk to you!"

He took a deep breath. "I'm not leaving until you open this door. Not if I have to sleep out here all night long."

He waited, and then the sound of the lock being turned caused him to smile. The door cracked open, and he could see her face. He could tell she was still angry by the set of her jaw and the fire in her eyes.

"What do you want?"

"I want you to forgive me for the things I said. I have no right to judge who you go out with. I should have kept my mouth shut, but I've been so glad to have you back in my life, I think I was afraid that might change if you got to know someone like Chip Holder. He's a war hero, and I'm just a cop, nobody important like him. I guess I was jealous."

The door opened wider, and her expression softened. "You are important, Ryan. The people of this city depend on you to help provide a safe place for them to live. You're important to Jamie because he depends on you to guide him to be the kind of man he needs to become. And you're important to me because I need your friendship."

Her words stirred his emotions and he felt the tightness in his chest begin to ease. "You're important to me, Jessica. I couldn't leave without telling you how sorry I am for the things I said. I won't interfere in your business again."

"I'm sorry for the way I talked to you also. Can

we please forget all we said and get back to feeling comfortable with each other again?"

"That's what I want."

He didn't know who moved first, but she was suddenly in his arms with her head resting against his chest. He sighed in contentment and pulled her closer. "Oh, Jessica. I don't want to ever argue with you again."

"Neither do I," she murmured. After a moment, she pulled back and stared up at him. "Ryan, what's happening between us?"

He shrugged. "I think time will tell, Jessica. But whatever it is, it feels so right."

She tightened her arms around his back and snuggled closer to him. "I think so, too."

ELEVEN

Two hours later, Jessica scooped the last bite of cheese-cake from her dessert plate and popped it in her mouth. She closed her eyes in ecstasy as the creamy morsel slid down her throat. Across the table Ryan raised his eyebrows in mock surprise and grinned.

"It's good to know you still have a healthy appetite," he said. "You always could hold your own with any of the guys at the precinct when it came to eating."

She wiped her mouth on her napkin and nodded. "It comes from growing up with two brothers who were always hungry. I don't know how my mom was able to keep enough food in the house for them."

Ryan laughed and took a sip of his coffee. "I haven't seen Adam in a long time. I wonder if he's going to dislike me as much as Lucas does."

"Lucas doesn't dislike you. It's just that he feels extra protective of me because we're twins. He always took care of me when we were in school, and he thinks he still has to do it. He doesn't realize that I'm all grown up."

Ryan let his gaze drift over her. "Yeah, you're certainly a grown-up lady. With a mind of your own and a tongue that can make a guy's ears curl."

She laughed and propped her hands on her hips. "And what about you, mister? If I remember correctly, you had a lot of things to say earlier today, too."

"Yeah, I did, and I hope you've forgiven me for that." He swept a hand over the empty dishes on the table in front of them. "After all, I did feed you."

"You did, and it was a delicious meal." She looked down at the jeans she wore. "At least you could have given me time to freshen up some, though. I've had these clothes on since this morning. They're not exactly what I'd wear to go out to a restaurant this fancy."

"Quit worrying about how you look. You're the prettiest woman in this place. All the guys keep looking this way, and it's beginning to bother me. Especially that guy over there."

He cut his eyes to the side, and she glanced in that direction. A man who appeared to be in his late thirties sat alone at a table, staring at her. When he realized he'd been caught, he dropped his gaze and directed his attention back to the steak in front of him.

Something about the way in which he'd been staring at her sent cold chills down her back, and she shivered. "Do you know him? I've never seen him before."

Ryan shook his head. "No, but if he's not careful, I'm going to have to go over there and have a little chat with him. Maybe he needs to be reminded it's not nice to stare at people in public."

She laughed then, and he grinned in reply. "This is the way I like it between us," she said. "It's so much better than fighting."

"I know. And I promise I'm not going to argue with you anymore."

She tilted her head to one side and frowned. "Are you sure about that?"

He shrugged. "Well, at least not until you make me angry again."

They both laughed at that, and her gaze strayed to the man sitting alone across the room. He looked back down at his plate when he realized she had caught him staring again. Jessica started to say something to Ryan, but they were having such a good time together she didn't want to spoil the mood.

Before she could say anything, Ryan pulled his cell phone from his pocket and frowned. "What's the matter?" she asked.

"Jamie still hasn't called me. I don't know whether to be worried or angry with him."

Jessica frowned. "Did you let him know that Lee Tucker is still at large?"

"I did. You'd think he would be more thoughtful of my feelings and let me know where he is."

Jessica reached across the table and grasped his hand. "He's still a kid, Ryan. He'll become more concerned with other people's feelings as he gets older. He seemed like a really nice guy when I met him the other day."

"He is, most of the time. But sometimes he drives me crazy. And he really liked you. A lot better than Lucas likes me."

She threw up her hands in protest. "There you go again. I keep telling you my brother likes you. It's me that he gets aggravated with."

Ryan stroked his chin and directed a smirk at her.

"Well, I can see how that would happen. I've had my share of aggravation, too."

She swatted his arm and frowned. "There you go criticizing me again. You'd better watch out or you're going to find yourself in big trouble with me."

He cringed as if afraid of her and laughed. "I certainly don't want that. Maybe I'd better take you home while I'm still ahead." He glanced at his cell phone. "And maybe Jamie will be back before I get home."

"I'm sure he will be."

Ryan signaled for the waitress to bring the check, and a few minutes later they were making their way through the dining room to the front door. When they stepped outside, Jessica was surprised to see that it had begun to rain while they were eating.

The rain beating down on the metal awning that ran across the front of the restaurant sounded like a drum line pounding out rhythms for a drill team. Jessica inhaled the scent of the rain as the downpour grew stronger.

They stood waiting for the rain to slack up, but it continued to fall hard enough that the water puddled in the street. After a few minutes, Ryan turned the collar up on his jacket and pulled his car keys from his pocket. "There's no need for you to get wet. I'll get the car and bring it around front to pick you up. Wait for me right here, and I'll pull up to the awning."

She nodded, and he ducked his head down in his collar as far as it would go before he took off at a run toward the parking lot. Behind her the restaurant door opened just as an SUV pulled up to the awning. The car's back door opened, as if waiting for someone to enter. She heard footsteps behind her and turned to look over her shoulder to see who had exited the restaurant.

Her eyes grew wide at the sight of the man who'd stared at her all through dinner. He strode toward her, his eyes blazing as if they were on fire. She turned to run, but before she could, he picked her up as if she weighed nothing, hoisted her over his shoulder and threw her in the backseat of the waiting car. She started to scream, but before she could, a cloth was stuffed in her mouth and secured with a band pulled tight around her face. He pushed her farther into the car and climbed in after her before the vehicle roared away.

She'd been tossed to the floor, and she could feel someone's feet next to her face. She struggled to sit up, but a slap across the face sent her reeling to the floorboard. Before she could move, the man who'd thrown her into the car grabbed her hands, pulled them up and secured them in front of her with zip ties. Another slap knocked her head against the floor.

"That's the start of payback for breaking my arm," a sinister voice muttered. "I could have hit you harder with the other hand, but that arm is in a sling, thanks to you."

Jessica's breath froze in her throat and her stomach churned in fear. She didn't have to see this man's face. She knew who had spoken. Lee Tucker.

Unable to move or make a sound, she curled into a ball and huddled away from the feet and legs of the two men who sat in the seat. Hot tears ran down her cheeks and she wondered if Ryan had discovered she was missing yet.

She had no idea where they were taking her and

wondered what awaited her when she arrived. All she could do was pray that somehow Ryan would find her.

Her legs began to cramp from the position she was in, and she tried to straighten them a bit. As she did, the side of her boot rubbed against the floorboard, and she almost gasped aloud. She had forgotten the GPS Ryan had given her this morning. In her haste to go to dinner with him, she hadn't changed clothes.

The tiny transmitter still lay tucked in her boot. She lay very still and began to pray that Ryan would be able to trace her whereabouts.

Ryan was nearly drenched by the time he arrived at his car. He jumped inside and shook himself like a big dog after finding shelter from a rainstorm. Water ran down his neck from his hair and trickled over his back.

A cold chill attacked him, and he shivered as he started the car and turned on the heater to try to dry out. He allowed the engine to idle a bit so the interior of the car would be warm when Jessica climbed in, but after a few minutes, he put the car in gear and drove to the restaurant entrance.

He frowned as he pulled up to the awning and didn't see her. Where was she? This was the place she'd been standing when he'd left to get the car. Maybe she'd forgotten something and had gone back inside to get it.

He slid the gearshift into Park but didn't turn off the engine. He turned on the radio and found his favorite rock station and settled back to wait for her to come back outside. After several minutes, he frowned. Why hadn't she returned?

With a sigh he turned off the engine, stepped out into the rain again and ran back inside the restaurant.

The hostess smiled when he entered. "Hello, sir. Did you forget something?"

He shook his head. "No, I'm looking for the young woman who was with me when I left. She was going to wait for me to bring the car around, but when I got to the awning, she was nowhere to be seen. Did she come back inside?"

The hostess shook her head. "I didn't see her, but I've been busy seating some latecomers. She could have gone into the restroom while I was away from my station. Would you like me to check and see if she's in there?"

"Would you, please? It's not like her to disappear this way."

The hostess smiled. "I'll be right back." The woman returned a few minutes later and shook her head. "I'm sorry. She's not in there."

He stared past her to the dining room. "Is it possible she could have gone back into the dining room?"

"I don't think so, sir, but you're welcome to look if you'd like."

Ryan strode into the dining room and let his gaze drift over the tables filled with diners. Soft music filled the room, and the buzz of quiet conversations provided a serene atmosphere for dining.

The table where he and Jessica had sat was empty now. So was the table where the man who'd stared at Jessica all through dinner had sat. His heart lurched and he rushed back to the hostess.

She looked up from the menus she was rearranging. "Did you find your friend?"

"No," he said, "but I wonder if you recall a man who ate alone at that table near the window. He had dark hair and was wearing a brown business suit."

She thought for a moment before she nodded. "You mean the man with the scar on his face?"

Ryan frowned. "I don't remember seeing a scar."

"He had one, that's for sure." She traced a finger from her ear down to the corner of her lip. "From here to here. I started to seat him at another table near the back so I could even out the tables the waitresses were assigned to, but he objected and said he wanted that one by the window. I thought it was probably so that the side of his face with the scar was turned toward the window and wasn't so noticeable."

"No, it was so he could keep an eye on us," Ryan whispered.

The hostess frowned. "I'm sorry. I didn't understand what you said."

"It's not important," he said. "Thank you for all your help."

He rushed from the restaurant, stopped underneath the awning and raked his hand through his hair. "Where are you, Jessica?" he muttered.

"You lookin' for that girl you was with?"

The voice from the darkness startled him, and he whirled to see who had spoken. His gaze lit on a ragged man curled up next to the building underneath the awning. A backpack lay next to him, and his clothes were wet. Ryan realized he had to be one of the numerous homeless people who roamed the streets of the city looking for a place to sleep each night.

He stepped closer to the man. "Yes. Did you see her?"

The man nodded. "I did. I saw that guy that took her, too."

Ryan's heart plummeted to the pit of his stomach. "Somebody took her?"

"Yeah. I seen you two come out. Then you went to get the car. Another car drove up, and this guy ran out of the restaurant, grabbed her and threw her in the car. They took off like they was being chased by dogs."

Ryan was shaking so badly he could hardly stand still. "What kind of car was it?"

"A big one," the man said.

Ryan groaned. "No, I mean, was it a two-door, a truck, a van? What?"

"It was one of those big ones that set up real high, and you climb up on a running board to get into."

"An SUV?"

The man nodded. "Yeah. That's what they call them. It was a black SUV."

Ryan pulled out his wallet, grabbed all the bills he had and handed them to the man. "Thanks for helping me. Go get yourself a good meal tonight."

The man nodded and gave Ryan a little salute. "I'll do that. I hope you find your lady friend."

"I do, too," Ryan muttered before he ran back to the car.

Once inside, he pulled out his cell phone and said a quick prayer that Jessica had not removed the GPS tracker. He punched the app and sighed with relief when her signal popped up on the screen.

He started the car and pulled into traffic. He had no idea where they were taking her, but as long as they didn't discover the tracker, he would be on their trail.

Then he'd decide how he was going to rescue her from whomever had taken her.

TWELVE

The car came to an abrupt halt, and Jessica lay still, barely daring to breathe. She had no idea where they were or even who had abducted her, with the exception of Lee Tucker. As the car doors began to open and the men inside stepped out, she listened in hopes of catching a hint in the conversation of what they were planning and how it involved her.

She could hear low voices outside the vehicle, but so far she couldn't determine how many there were. One of the voices rose in pitch as if the speaker had become angry, and she wondered if it was Lee Tucker.

After a few minutes, the conversation lulled, and one of the car's back doors reopened. The person who'd opened it stood near her head, but she didn't try to raise herself so she could see his face. Then suddenly, strong hands gripped her under the arms and pulled her out of the car. She landed in a rain puddle on the pavement with a thump, her head next to the back tire of the SUV.

"Where do you want me to take her?" the man who'd tossed her to the ground asked.

"Inside with the other one."

Her heart leaped into her throat. The other one? Had they also taken Ryan captive? If so, there was no hope for them to escape. Her only chance had been that Ryan would come to her rescue.

The man bent down and dragged her to her feet. The rain had stopped, but the sky was overcast. She glanced around to try to determine where she was, but she didn't recognize any landmarks.

She stood in what appeared to be a parking lot next to a large building that could have once been used as a warehouse. The sound of rolling water drifted across a low bluff in the distance, and she wondered if they were near the Mississippi River. There were no lights around the outside of the building, although she could see light shining through a few windows.

The man who'd pulled her to her feet shoved her toward the building, and she stumbled but regained her footing before she fell. She stared up into the face of the man who'd watched her in the restaurant. There, she'd caught sight of only his left profile, but now in the dim light, she could make out a scar that ran from the edge of his mouth to the tip of his right ear. It must have been a terrible knife injury to leave such a scar.

He pushed her again, and she staggered through the door and emerged into a huge room that at one time must have been the main floor of the warehouse. Several doors to what she assumed were small offices lined the wall, and he pointed to one about midway into the building.

She walked toward it and paused outside as he reached around her to unlock it. He opened the door and shoved her inside, relocking it before she could turn around. The room was pitch-black, but she could hear labored breathing coming from near the far wall.

She wanted to call out, but the gag in her mouth prevented that. She raised her bound hands up to her face and pulled at the gag until it slipped out of her mouth and dangled around her neck.

Next she leaned against the wall and tried to pull her hands apart. It took only a few seconds to determine that her abductor had tightened the zip ties as much as they could be. But it took several minutes of maneuvering her wrists to get the locking mechanism to move so that it was positioned directly between her two hands. Taking a big breath and holding her bound wrists in front of her, she lifted her arms above her head and brought them down in one quick motion into her stomach while flaring her elbows out like chicken wings. Just as she knew they would, the zip ties broke at their weakest point—the locking mechanism.

With the ties off her wrists, it took only a few seconds more to untie the band hanging around her neck. Once free of her restraints, she reached up and rubbed her cheek where she had received two blows. No doubt there would be bruises. That was if she was able to get out of here alive.

A rustling sound near the far wall reminded her she wasn't alone, and she took a tentative step toward the movement. "Hello," she said in a low voice. "Is there anybody here?"

"I'm here." The words came out garbled and strained but somehow familiar.

She reached out to search for obstacles in her path as she took one hesitant step after another toward the wall. Her foot hit the edge of a chair, and she jerked to a halt. Her eyes were beginning to adjust to the darkness, and she strained to make out the figure tied to the chair.

"Who are you?" she asked.

"Jamie Spencer," the voice answered. "Who are you?"

Jessica clamped her hand over her mouth to keep from screaming out loud and dropped to her knees beside the chair. "Jamie, it's Jessica Knight," she whispered. "What are you doing here?"

"Jessica? I'm glad to see you." He paused a moment. "Or maybe I shouldn't be. If you're here, then that means you're in as much trouble as I am."

"I'm all right, but how about you? Are you hurt?"

"My head hurts where they hit me," Jamie answered. "And my hands are numb from being tied to this chair."

"Let me see if I can help with that."

Jessica reached up to touch his forehead, and her hand came away sticky. From the feel of his wet skin, he'd lost a lot of blood. Might still be bleeding, for all she could tell here in the dark. She moved behind the chair and began to work at the ropes binding him. It took several minutes, but she was finally able to free him.

He pulled his arms in front of him and began to flex his fingers. "I wish I had something to tie around your head," she said, "but the only thing I've got is the cloth they stuffed in my mouth. I don't think it would be a good idea to use it." She felt his head again, this time more thoroughly, and it didn't feel as if any fresh blood was seeping out.

Jamie finished flexing his fingers and reached down to untie his feet, then pushed into a standing position. "That feels better."

"I'm glad, but tell me what happened to you. Ryan has been worried to death because you hadn't called."

"I knew he would be, and I'm sorry about that. I was on my way home this afternoon and stopped at a deserted rest stop for a few minutes. This van drove up, and before I knew it, I'd been hit over the head and thrown inside. This is where they brought me. What about you?"

"They abducted me from a restaurant when Ryan went to the parking lot to get the car. I have no idea where we are, but I'm hopeful Ryan will be able to find us."

She started to tell him about the GPS tracking device in her boot but thought better of it. There was no need to get his hopes up. After all, it might not even function properly or she might be out of range or something else could go wrong.

"Do you think he can?" Jamie asked.

"Let's pray he does," she replied. "But tell me what you've been investigating for the past few days. Ellie told us about your meeting with Gerald Price and that he was a private investigator working for the Harveys to dig into their son's and daughter-in-law's deaths."

"When I saw that he'd been murdered, I decided to go talk to the two senate candidates. While I was at Senator Mitchum's office, I overheard his chief of staff and another guy talking about Gerald and how they couldn't afford for anything about the Harveys' murders to be linked to them. I tried to slip away without their knowing I'd overheard, but they saw me. The guy talking to Mr. Stark chased me, but I got away."

"Had you ever seen him before?"

Jamie shook his head. "I don't know. I didn't get a good look at him. But the next day when I got home after the convenience-store robbery, I got to thinking about what the robber had said about me sticking my nose in where it didn't belong. That's when I realized that guy at the store had intended to kill me. He would have, too, if it hadn't been for you. I knew it had to be somehow related to what I'd overheard at Senator Mitchum's office. That's when I got the idea to go to Atlanta to see the Harveys."

"How did your visit with them go?"

"I told them what I overheard at Senator Mitchum's office, and they said that Cal and Susan were working on a story about a big drug organization that was active in the eastern part of the state. Whoever was the head of it had partnered with some local police officers who helped them keep one step ahead of the law. They were just about to publish their story and name the head of the organization when they were killed. Their computers and all their research were taken from their home, and a gang member was accused of killing them. But the Harveys thought it was somebody up in the drug organization who had ordered the hits."

"We learned some things about the case after you disappeared," Jessica said.

"What kind of things?"

"Well, for one, we learned that the guy who robbed the convenience store is a hit man and that his DNA was found at the Harveys' murder scene. He also broke into my apartment to kill me, but Ryan prevented that. On his way to jail, the police who were escorting him were killed, and he escaped. Ryan and I learned, too, that he has been seen at Senator Mitchum's offices by someone other than you. So it stands to reason he's working for the senator."

"I'm not so sure about that," Jamie said.

"Why not?"

"Because the Harveys knew what county their son thought the drug organization had its headquarters and where he was concentrating his investigation. That's where I went before I came home, and I found out some interesting facts."

Jessica's eyes had grown large. "Such as?"

"Such as it's the home county of Chip Holder. When he was rescued from that terrorist group six years ago, he went back home but he never got a job. He started touring the country doing speaking engagements instead. I started researching how much he made. At first he charged high speaking fees, and people paid it. But after a while the public began to lose interest and he couldn't book many appearances. The money he was making wasn't enough to support the kind of lifestyle he'd started living. You should see his house. It has to be worth millions. The money for it had to come from somewhere. But there wasn't any record of his earning enough for something like that."

"How did he afford it?" Jessica asked.

"That's what I wondered. So I talked to a lot of the old-timers in the community. Some of them were closemouthed, but a few liked talking to a reporter.

They said he inherited a lot of money when his wife died."

With all Jessica had been hearing for the past few minutes, she didn't think anything else would surprise her. But this latest revelation did. "Wife? I didn't know he had a wife who died."

"Yeah, according to the folks I talked to, she committed suicide soon after he came home from the military. Her family was rich, and he inherited all her money."

This story was becoming more bizarre by the moment. "How did she commit suicide?"

"Killed herself with his shotgun while he was at church one Sunday. But one old fellow told me that things hadn't been too good between them since he came home. She had decided to have him declared legally dead so she could marry her new boyfriend. Then he showed up alive, and she wanted a divorce. But she killed herself before she could file." Jamie paused a minute. "I'm feeling dizzy. I think I'll sit down."

He sank back down in the chair, and Jessica sat down on the floor next to him. She wrapped her hands around her knees. "This is all interesting, Jamie, but it's gossip not evidence. We know for sure that Lee Tucker, the man who tried to kill both you and me, is connected to Senator Mitchum. What we have to do is figure out how."

"I don't know about that either, Jessica. I—" He stopped talking when they heard the door open.

Someone flipped a switch outside the door and the room flooded with light. Jessica staggered to her feet and shielded her eyes from the sudden blinding flash. She heard footsteps and squinted to see who had entered. Her mouth dropped open at the sight of Wendell Stark standing inside the door, with Lee Tucker right behind him.

"Well, what do we have here? Two nosy people who want to meddle in things that don't concern them." Wendell Stark glanced at Jamie. "You should have left well enough alone, young man. And you, Miss Knight, should have passed on this bounty. It's going to end up costing you dearly."

Jessica clenched her fists at her sides and glared at Wendell as he and Lee stepped into the room. "Whatever you have planned for us, you'd better reconsider. You two, along with Senator Mitchum, have made too many mistakes, starting with the murders of Cal and Susan Harvey. If you harm Jamie and me, you're going to end up having the police and everybody at the Knight Agency on your trail. By the time they get through, all three of you will be sharing a cell in the state prison."

Wendell stared at her a minute and then glanced at Lee before he threw back his head and burst out laughing. "That's the funniest thing I've heard in a long time."

"You'll be laughing out of the other side of your mouth before my family gets through with you," she ground out.

Wendell shook his head as he struggled to quit laughing. "I don't think so."

"And why not?" Jessica demanded.

Jamie pushed to his feet and grasped her by the arm. "Jessica, there's something else I was just getting ready to tell you."

She whirled and stared at Jamie. "What is it?"

He swallowed and darted a glance at Wendell. "I was going to say that I also found out that Wendell Stark was Chip Holder's best friend when they were kids. They grew up on adjoining farms."

Jessica's mouth dropped open. "They did what?"

"You heard him," a voice said from the door. "Best friends since childhood, business partners for years and both determined to make it to the White House no matter who gets in our way."

Jessica shrank back from the sight of Chip Holder leaning against the door frame, his arms crossed and a half smile on his face. "Including Senator Mitchum?" she asked.

Chip nodded and straightened to glare at her. "As well as you two and that nosy boyfriend of yours. None of you are going to stand in my way."

Following the flashing signal on his phone app, Ryan pulled his car to a stop in a wooded area just past the deserted warehouse where the GPS indicated Jessica had been brought. He turned off the car's headlights and checked the address the tracker displayed on his cell phone before he punched in the number for Dispatch.

When the dispatcher answered, he identified himself by his badge number and quickly relayed all the information about where he was. "I need backup immediately," he said.

"They're on their way," the dispatcher responded. "ETA four minutes."

"Good. I'm going to move closer," he said and disconnected the call.

He crouched low as he ran from the spot where he'd parked the car and headed toward the building. As he made his way through the trees toward the building, he suddenly caught sight of movement at the back. He stopped behind a big oak and pressed himself against the trunk. Gripping his gun with both hands, he peered around the tree and spotted a man holding a gun at the rear of the building. A guard, no doubt.

Ryan squatted and felt around on the ground until his fingers touched a stick from one of the branches. Grasping it tightly, he eased back to a standing position and threw it past the guard and into the trees beyond. The man jerked to attention when the stick struck the ground, and he whirled with his gun pointed in the direction of the sound.

Ryan charged like a madman from his hiding place and brought his gun down on the back of the man's head. With a slight moan, the guard crumpled to the ground. Ryan had the man's gun stuffed in his waistband and his hands cuffed behind his back within seconds.

He turned the guard's head and leaned closer to see if he recognized him. The man from the restaurant. For the first time, he caught sight of the scar the hostess had told him about.

Satisfied that the man would be disabled until the police arrived, Ryan rose to his feet and peered around the side of the building at the SUV parked near an entrance. That had to be the vehicle the homeless man had seen at the restaurant. Jessica had to be inside this abandoned warehouse.

He was just about to move toward the entrance

of the building when the headlights of a car swept across the paved parking lot. He ducked back behind the building and peered around the corner as the car came to a stop.

A man climbed out and headed for the door. He opened it and paused to drop a lit cigarette butt to the ground before entering. That short hesitation on his part was enough time for the light from inside to shine across his features and reveal his identity to Ryan.

Chip Holder. What was he doing here?

Ryan waited until Chip had entered the building. Then he wrapped both hands around his gun and crept forward. He grasped the door handle and eased the door open inch by inch until he could peer inside. He could hear voices in the distance but saw no one in the large room that he thought must have once been the main work area of the warehouse.

Careful to make no sound, he squeezed through the opening of the door and stepped inside. To his left he could see light pouring out a doorway and could hear voices coming from within. He held the gun with both hands in front of him as he flattened himself against the wall and slid toward the open door.

When he arrived at the door, he stopped and listened. His heart raced at the sound of Jessica's voice coming from inside. He could not, however, make out what she was saying.

He frowned and took a step closer as another voice spoke. When he recognized it, he froze, and his hand trembled. Jamie! And he was saying something about Wendell Stark and Chip Holder being best friends since childhood.

But the biggest surprise came when he heard Chip

Holder speak as clearly as if he stood next to him. "Best friends since childhood, business partners for years and both determined to make it to the White House no matter who gets in our way."

Ryan recognized the determination in the voice. He'd known other men equally focused on an end, men who'd become desperate to achieve their goals. They'd let nothing stop them. And right now, his brother and Jessica were in Chip Holder and Wendell Stark's way. Chills cascaded over his body as he fought the image of what the men could and would do to them.

Ryan glanced down at his watch. Where was his backup? They should have gotten here by now.

He returned his attention to the conversation in the room, his knees growing weak at the next words he heard Chip say. "Okay, Lee. We've got to get rid of these two. You and Wendell take them over to Mitchum's headquarters and leave their bodies where they'll be found. Wendell, did you get Mitchum's gun?"

"I did. We'll use it for these two. And I put that sedative in his drink earlier. So he should be out until morning with no recollection of anything that happened tonight. No memory, and no alibi."

Chip laughed. "Good job. Now, get going."

Ryan couldn't wait any longer. He had to act immediately. He took a deep breath and stepped into the doorway. "Hands up! You're all under arrest."

Lee Tucker spun around and he pulled a gun from the sling that held his left arm against his chest. Ryan fired first, and Lee dropped to the ground. Before Ryan could reach the gun that had fallen onto the floor, Wendell Stark scooped it up and pointed it at Ryan.

Ryan whirled to cover Wendell, but Chip's voice called out, "Drop your gun, Spencer, unless you want to see these two die."

Ryan jerked his gaze back to Chip and nearly groaned in dismay to see him standing behind Jessica and Jamie with a gun in his hand. He pointed it first at Jessica's head and then Jamie's.

"Which one will I shoot first?" he said. "But I don't guess it really matters because I intend to kill both of them before we leave here."

Ryan clutched his gun tighter and glared at Chip. "Give it up, Holder. The police are on their way. You can't get out of this one."

Chip smiled. "Oh, I think I still can." He glanced at Wendell and shrugged. "Sorry, Wendell."

Jessica screamed as Chip fired. Surprise flashed across Wendell's face before he toppled facedown with blood pouring from his chest.

"Why did you do that?" Ryan asked.

"Because I still intend to come out the winner," Chip said. He glanced around the room. "I need to get out of here before your friends arrive. So I have to kill you three and make my escape now. Tomorrow I think I'll call a press conference to express my shock at how Senator Mitchum's chief of staff and a known hit man who's wanted for multiple murders had a shoot-out with a police officer trying to rescue his brother and girlfriend from their clutches. I may even shed a tear or two for you."

Jessica clenched her fists at her sides. "You'll never get away with this."

"Oh, yes I will," he said.

Ryan almost gasped at the transformation that overcame Chip's face so suddenly. Instead of the candidate who portrayed himself as a war hero and patriot who'd come from humble beginnings, Chip Holder suddenly looked like a rabid dog.

"I'm going to get away with it because this country owes me," he hissed.

Ryan frowned and inched a bit closer. "Owes you for what?"

"Five years of my life was spent in a dark hole by myself unless I was taken out and beaten by the terrorist group that held me prisoner. And during that time my country didn't lift a hand to rescue me. They let me rot there for five years before they showed up. But it just got worse when I came home. My old job was gone. My wife didn't want me anymore. And I had no money." He chuckled under his breath. "So I set out to change things. First off, I took care of my wife."

"So you killed her and made it look like suicide," Jamie said.

"You got that right. She paid for not standing by me. Wendell was the only one who stuck by me. It didn't take us long to know that drugs could make us some money, and we built a thriving drug trade. But it was nothing like what I decided I really wanted— the biggest job in the country. The White House. And Wendell was going to help me get it. The only problem was, I had no experience in politics. So I began to contribute to the local party, then to elections." He chuckled. "It's really funny how many people are in office today because my drug money helped them get there, and they don't even know it."

Ryan took another step closer. If he could keep Chip talking, maybe the backup would arrive. "So you wormed your way into the good graces of people wanting to make a difference by serving their country in elected office."

"Yeah. And I began to get on committees, and before long the big boys in the state were talking about getting me elected to office. And that's how I became the party's candidate to run against Mitchum."

Ryan inched closer. "But you couldn't leave it to the voters to decide who was best qualified. You decided to sabotage Mitchum's campaign by getting Wendell hired by Senator Mitchum, and the two of you set out to steal his senate seat as a stepping-stone to the White House." Ryan had figured it all out. "Your big mistake was hiring Lee Tucker for your hit man."

Chip shook his head. "We were surprised when those murders came back to haunt us. We thought we'd set Tommie Oakes up with enough evidence that we'd never have to worry about it again." He took a breath. "Those Harveys had discovered we were in the drug business, and they were about to print their story. We had to get rid of them, but old man Harvey just wouldn't let it go. Even after four years he hired that investigator to find out the truth. By that time we were getting too close to the senate seat and couldn't allow those murders to resurface."

"So you killed Gerald Price."

Chip shrugged. "Lee did." Then he frowned and pointed the gun at Jamie's head. "And then you had to stick your nose into it. A college kid, out to get a story, wasn't about to interfere with my plan to go to Washington."

Ryan's breath caught in his throat at the sight of the gun pointed at his brother's head. He had to keep Chip talking. "Don't make matters worse for yourself, Chip. It's all over for you. There's no way you can get out of here. The list of charges against you are so long that you won't see the outside of a jail cell ever again."

Chip's eyes blazed, and he jerked the gun away from Jamie and pressed it against Jessica's head. "It's not over. If I survived that hole I lived in for five years, I can get out of this situation. My country owes me for what it took away from me, and I intend to get it back."

Ryan's mind was reeling as he tried to think of a way to disarm Chip. "There's no getting anything back, Chip." Then a thought popped into his head, and he stared at Jessica. Just as she'd called upon an event of their past to alert him about the killer behind the door in her apartment, he would do the same. "Just like with us, Jessica," he told her, putting his plan into action. "I wish we could get back that feeling we had the time we celebrated with Rafe Johnson."

He knew she understood his reference to the bank hostage situation when her eyes sparkled, and she smiled. "I do, too."

"All right, you two," Chip roared, "that's enough—"

He didn't finish his sentence because the moment his mouth opened, Jessica whirled and delivered a hammer-fist punch to the side of Chip's face just below the ear, right at the point where the nerve endings traveled to the brain. A shocked look spread across Chip's paralyzed features as his gun clattered to the floor. Ryan surged forward at the same instant and threw his entire weight into Chip's body. Together they fell to the floor with Ryan on top.

Before Chip could move, Jessica had his gun and was pointing it at him. "Don't move, Chip, or I'll fire."

Ryan grabbed the gun that he'd lost in the scuffle and jumped to his feet. Together he and Jessica hauled Chip to his feet just as backup burst into the room. Ryan pulled his jacket back to reveal the badge on his belt as the first officer in the door took in the scene.

"Detective Ryan Spencer," he said. "This is my brother, and this is Jessica Knight, former police officer and a fugitive recovery agent with the Knight Agency. The man we're holding here is Chip Holder, candidate for the United States Senate." He pointed to Wendell. "That's Wendell Stark. Holder also shot him, but I shot the other man. His name is Lee Tucker. He's a hired hit man. We need to see if both of them are still alive."

One of the officers who'd entered the room dropped to his knees and placed his fingers on Wendell's pulse, then did the same with Lee. After a moment, he spoke into his lapel mic. "We need an ambulance at the old Riverside Warehouse. We have two wounded men here."

Jessica took a step closer. "I thought they were both dead."

The officer shook his head. "No, but they need to get to a hospital as soon as possible."

Ryan jerked his head in Chip's direction. "He needs to be placed under arrest right now. I guess we can sort all the charges out after we get him to the station. They are too numerous to mention at the moment."

The officer nodded to the uniformed cop next to him. "Cuff him and take him downtown. And call the crime-scene squad along with homicide investigators. From the looks of things, we're in for a long night."

As Chip was being led away in handcuffs, Ryan called out to the police officer, "Oh, by the way, there's another guy at the rear of the building. He may still be unconscious."

The officer in charge of the scene turned to Ryan. "We're going to need a statement from all of you. Don't leave until we give you permission."

Ryan nodded. "We won't, but Miss Knight and my brother have been through quite an ordeal tonight. Is it okay for us to have some time alone to enjoy having come through this in one piece?"

"Sure," he said. "Go find a quiet place somewhere and relax for a while. We'll call you when we need to talk with you."

Ryan walked over and put one arm around his brother and the other around Jessica. For a moment he thought his knees were going to collapse from the relief he was feeling, but he forced himself to stand still. He hugged them both, then guided them toward the door.

Thank You, God, for bringing us through this experience safely, he prayed.

He glanced down, and Jessica was smiling up at him. He hugged her tighter and repeated the prayer he'd just offered up.

THIRTEEN

Three hours later, Jessica watched from across the hospital room as Ellie sat by Jamie's bed grasping his hand, and Ryan hovered over his brother on the other side. The look of relief that lined Ryan's face brought a smile to Jessica's lips. No longer was he worried about his brother and the fear Jamie's rash actions had caused all of them to feel.

A big bandage covered the wound on Jamie's head, but he appeared to have recovered his strength after the loss of so much blood. In fact, Jamie was already fussing that he had to spend the night in the hospital.

"Why can't I go back to my apartment? I feel fine."

Ryan sighed and shook his head. "I've told you at least ten times. The doctor thinks they need to keep you overnight for observation. If all goes well, which he has assured me he thinks it will, you can go home in the morning."

Jamie pounded his fists into the mattress. "But I have a story to write. I need to be doing that now, while everything is still fresh in my memory."

Ellie arched an eyebrow and directed a stern look in Jamie's direction. "I'll help you do that in the morning.

Now, do as the doctor and your brother say and take it easy. The sooner you cooperate, the sooner they'll let you out of here."

Jamie growled and settled back against the pillows, then smiled in Ellie's direction. "Yes, ma'am, if you say so. I never realized how bossy you can be."

She grasped his hand tighter and blinked at the tears filling her eyes. "Oh, Jamie, I was so worried about you. Don't you ever scare me like that again."

Jamie's eyes softened, and he brought her hand up to his mouth and kissed her knuckles. "Don't worry. I won't."

Ryan cleared his throat. "And that goes for me, too."

Jamie glanced at Ryan. "Okay, big brother. But I still have a lot of questions about what happened tonight. Have you talked to your friends at the precinct to see what's going on?"

Ryan nodded. "I have. Wendell Stark and Lee Tucker are both in surgery right now. It looks like they'll both live to face the charges against them. Mac and I will meet with the DA in the morning to discuss the evidence against them and Chip Holder for the Harvey murders as well as those of Richard Parker and Kenny Macey. Then there's the attempted murders of you and Jessica."

"And what about Senator Mitchum?" Jamie asked.

"The police went to his house. When they couldn't get anybody to the door, they went in and found him asleep. His wife was out of town, so he was home alone. An ambulance brought him here to the hospital, where it was determined he'd been drugged. He's been admitted for observation, too."

Jamie's eyes grew large, and he pushed up on his elbows. "When I overheard that conversation at Senator Mitchum's campaign headquarters, I never dreamed it would lead to all this." He was quiet for a moment, and then he looked up at Ryan. "What about Tommie Oakes? What's going to happen to him now?"

Ryan shook his head. "I don't know. That will be up to the district attorney, but I think we have enough evidence for a judge to look at his case again. In the meantime, you need to concentrate on following doctor's orders and settle down."

Jessica laughed, rose from where she was sitting and stepped up beside the bed. "You'd better listen to your brother, Jamie. He can be a formidable foe when you oppose him. I've had experience firsthand with that."

Ryan looked at her from the opposite side of the bed, and his gaze, which seemed remote and a bit cold, sent a sudden warning through her body. They had barely had time to talk since he'd rescued her and Jamie, and she wanted some time alone with him. But so far, Ryan had made no effort to talk with her except to ask if she was all right. All his attention seemed to have shifted to his brother. At first, that had seemed reasonable to her, but now she was beginning to wonder. It seemed he was keeping a distance between them.

Ryan didn't say anything or even smile at her feeble attempt at humor. He simply glanced away from her and back to Jamie. What was the matter with him? she thought. He was treating her like a stranger.

After a moment, Jamie cleared his throat and reached

over to push the button that lowered the head of the bed to a reclining position.

"Look, you two," he said. "I think you have things to talk about, and I don't want to keep you. I'll be fine. So, Ryan, go on and take Jessica home. I promise I'll behave until you come back in the morning."

Indecision flickered across Ryan's face, but he shook his head. "I don't want to leave you."

"Don't worry," Ellie said. "I'll stay with him. You go on and take Jessica home."

Jessica could sense that Ryan didn't want to leave his brother. Or maybe he didn't want to be alone with her. If that was the case, she could make it easy for him. "Don't worry about getting me home, Ryan. All my family is waiting at my apartment for me to get there. I'll just call Lucas to come get me. Or maybe Adam. He and Claire got home tonight."

"I didn't know you'd called your family. When did you do that?" Ryan asked.

"While you were talking with the doctor. Really, it's no problem at all for one of them to run down here. That way I don't have to inconvenience you."

She tried to control the shaking in her voice, but she could hear the trembling caused by this sudden change in Ryan's attitude toward her. He had been aloof ever since they'd walked out of that room at the warehouse after the police arrived. As the minutes had passed, she had felt him distancing himself from her. Now, as she stared at him across Jamie's bed, she felt a chasm so wide between them that she feared the closeness they'd shared at dinner earlier could never again be reached.

"Taking you home won't be an inconvenience, but…" Ryan began.

Jamie stared first at her and then back at his brother. After a moment, he yawned. "Aw, take her on home, Ryan. And, Ellie, you need to go home, too. All I want is to get some sleep, and I can't do it with all of you here."

Jessica waited for Ryan to speak. When he didn't, she pulled out her cell phone. Her family had been worried sick about what she'd experienced tonight, and she needed to get home. There was no need to put off the happy reunion while she waited for Ryan Spencer to decide if he wanted to be alone with her or not.

She pulled her gaze away from Ryan, clutched her cell phone tighter and punched in Lucas's number. He answered on the first ring.

"Jessica? Are you on your way home?" She could hear the tenseness in his voice.

"Not yet. I need a ride. Can you come get me?"

He hesitated for a moment. "I thought you said Spencer was going to bring you home."

"No. Plans have changed."

"Of course I can come. Where will you be?"

"Come to the front entrance of the hospital. I'll be watching for you."

"Okay. I'm on my way."

She disconnected the call and slipped her cell phone in her pocket before she smiled back down at Jamie. "I'm glad you came through all this okay. But from now on, don't go off to chase a story without letting someone know where you are. Your brother has been crazy with worry over you."

Jamie cocked an eyebrow and glanced at his brother. "Yeah, I guess 'crazy' describes him sometimes." He grasped Jessica's hand. "Thanks for saving my life two times now. I'll never forget you."

She felt tears beginning to well in her eyes, and she blinked. "I won't forget you, either. Now, take care of yourself."

Ellie stood up and grabbed her coat. "If Ryan is determined to stay, I might as well go on home. I have a test in the morning, and I still need to study." She leaned over Jamie and planted a swift kiss on his lips. "I'll come back in the morning after my class and drive you home."

Jamie stared up at her and squeezed her hand. "I'd like that."

She walked over to Jessica as she turned to leave, and they had just reached the door when Ryan called out, "Jessica, wait."

He came around the end of Jamie's bed and stopped beside her. "I want to thank you, too. It's been great being back with you these past few days. Like I said, you always were the best partner I ever had."

He looked away, as if the words had taken a toll on him. Then he said, "Since Lee Tucker survived the gunshot wound, you have your fugitive in custody. I guess…" He paused and licked his lips. "I guess everything turned out all right for you after all."

She waited for him to say something else. To tell her being with her had made him realize how important she was to him. That he loved her. But he didn't speak. And she couldn't voice the words she wanted to say.

How could she tell him that those years of telling

herself she hated him were only because she felt betrayed by the man she'd come to love? And how could she tell him now that her love for him had never died but had been reborn with new hopes and dreams that this time the ending for them would be different than it had been before?

Evidently, he didn't feel the same, or he would say so. To him she was just a partner he'd once worked with. One who had saved his brother's life in a convenience-store holdup and then worked alongside him to bring down one of the country's most decorated war veterans.

As he stood staring at her, not moving or saying the things she wanted to hear, she realized she and Ryan were about to reach the end of the road. Everything that had once been between them was coming to a close. And he seemed ready to let it go. In one swift move, she bent down, slid her jeans leg up over her boot and pulled the GPS tracker out.

She held it up, and he opened his hand for her to drop it in his palm. It hit with a slight thump, and she took a deep breath.

"Like you said, I have my fugitive in custody and your brother is back safely. I guess this really ends our partnership," she said and whirled to leave the room.

The tears were streaming down her face by the time she reached the elevator, but she didn't look back. She didn't know how she would do it, but she was never going to look back again.

Ryan's fingers curled around the GPS tracker, and he watched as Jessica and Ellie stepped onto the elevator. The doors slid shut, and he had to prop his hand against the door frame of the hospital room to keep from sinking to his knees. He felt as if his heart had just shattered into a million pieces. He needed to be alone.

He glanced back over his shoulder at his brother. "I think I'll go get a cup of coffee. Can I bring you anything?"

"No, thanks."

Ryan nodded and hurried down the hall to the room where he'd seen some vending machines earlier. He purchased a cup of coffee and sank down on a battered vinyl sofa. He didn't know how long he sat there staring into his cup, but quite a bit of time must have passed. When he finally took a sip, the coffee had grown cold. He tossed the cup into a trash can and headed back to his brother's room.

When he reentered the hospital room, Jamie was sitting propped up in the bed, pillows behind his back and his arms crossed over his chest. "Feel better?"

"Yeah," Ryan muttered.

Jamie arched an eyebrow. "You never were a good liar, and you haven't changed. I guess tonight you've finally proved that you're as crazy as I always thought you were."

Ryan frowned and jerked his head up to stare at his brother. "What are you talking about?"

"Jessica, that's what. Anybody can see that you're in love with her. Why did you let her walk out of here like that without telling her?"

Ryan slipped the GPS into his pocket and then raked his hand through his hair. "I don't think it would ever work out between us. It's better that we end it now rather than later, when it will hurt even more. I need to get out of her life so she can be happy."

Jamie's mouth gaped open. "What are you talking about? Can't you see how much she loves you? It's written all over her face."

Ryan shook his head. "You don't know how I hurt her years ago. She says she's forgiven me, but I doubt if her family could ever put it behind them and accept me. I can't say that I blame them. I treated her really badly, and her twin brother hates me. Lucas looks at me like he wants to tear me limb from limb every time I see him."

"What does Jessica say about that?"

Ryan shrugged. "She says he likes me, that he's just very protective of her."

"Like you are of me?" Jamie asked.

Ryan couldn't help but smile. "Yeah, I guess so."

Jamie was quiet for a moment. "And have you asked Jessica to forgive you for how you treated her before?"

"I have, and she says she has. But how can I be sure? She's a stubborn woman, and I'm afraid the first time I disappoint her, she'll hate me again."

Jamie rolled his eyes and exhaled a deep breath. "Oh, brother. You are a piece of work. I thought you told me the reason you started going to that Bible study and became a believer was because of what you saw in her life."

"I did."

Jamie sat up in the bed. "So if she believes what the Bible says and lives her life that way, what makes you think she'd take back the forgiveness she gave you?"

"Well, I just thought—"

"No, you weren't thinking. You're scared. Maybe not so much of Jessica as you are of her family."

"Jamie, I think..."

"No," Jamie interrupted him. "You're not thinking. You remember how it was with Mom and Dad, and you're afraid that if Jessica's family doesn't like you, they'll cut her out of their lives like Mom's parents did her."

Ryan raked his hand through his hair. "And we both know how miserable she was. Every Christmas she hoped they'd at least call, but they never did. She gave up her whole family because she loved Dad, but I won't do that. I won't make Jessica choose between them and me."

Jamie leaned back against the pillows and shook his head in amazement. "I can't believe this. My big brother stormed into a warehouse by himself tonight and took on four bad guys to save me and the woman he loves. After meeting Jessica, I can't imagine her family would be anything like those men. Which leads me to ask this question. Have you asked them if they would have any objection to you?"

Ryan's face warmed, and he swallowed hard. "Well, no. But it just stands to reason..."

Jamie held up his hand. "Stop making excuses. Just because our mother's family has rejected us all our lives doesn't mean that Jessica's family is like them. Go talk with them. Tell them how you feel, and hear what they have to say."

Ryan shook his head in disbelief. "When did you get to be so smart?"

Jamie smiled. "Ever since I moved in with my big

brother and knew I wanted to grow up to be like him. Now go see Jessica's family."

Ryan let all Jamie had said drift through his mind as he weighed the arguments he'd been presented with. Then he smiled and punched his brother on the shoulder. "You're going to make a great investigative reporter. You know how to ask the right questions and get to the bottom of a problem."

Jamie grinned. "Thanks. Now, what are you going to do?"

He headed to the door. "I'm going to Jessica's apartment right now. Her family is there, and I'm going to talk to them. Then I'm going to throw myself on my knees and beg her to forgive me for being a stubborn fool. Then I'm going to ask her to marry me."

"Good luck," Jamie called as Ryan went out the door.

Ryan got to the elevator just as the doors opened. He swallowed and took a step back as he found himself staring into the angry face of Lucas Knight. He backed away another step as Jessica's brother came toward him, his fists clenched at his sides and a snarl pulling at his mouth.

Before Lucas could open his mouth, Ryan spoke up. "Lucas, I was just coming to see you. In fact, I want to talk to your whole family."

Lucas squinted and tilted his head. "That's funny. Because I came back here to talk to you, too."

"What about?" Ryan asked.

"My sister," Lucas hissed. "You broke her heart once, and I thought she'd finally gotten over you. Then you come back into her life, and she falls for you again. But just like last time, you toss her aside and break her heart."

Ryan held up his hands in front of him and shook his head. "No, it isn't like that. I love her. In fact, I want to marry her, but I didn't think your family approved of me. I didn't want to do anything to harm the relationship she has with all of you."

Lucas's eyes widened in a stunned expression. "What makes you think you could harm her relationship with us?"

"I know I hurt Jessica, and I don't blame your family for disliking me. But I want all of you to know that I love her with all my heart, and I hope you'll forgive me for hurting her. If she'll let me, I'd like to spend the rest of my life making it up to her for how I acted four years ago. I realize, though, that it may not be that easy for all of you to get past your feelings about me."

Lucas stared at Ryan for a few moments before he said anything. Then he exhaled. "We know you hurt her, but we want her to be happy. Which means that we will support any decision she makes about who she loves."

Ryan shook his head in disbelief. "You mean, I've been worried about nothing?"

Lucas laughed and slapped him on the shoulder. "It looks like it. Why didn't you tell me this when you brought Jessica to my house?"

Ryan shrugged. "I don't know. At the time I thought Jessica might not feel the same way. And she still may not, for all I know."

Lucas's eyebrows arched. "Not feel the same way?

Anybody with half a brain can see that she's head over heels in love with you. Are you blind?"

Ryan nodded. "I guess I am. I thought I was doing her a favor by getting out of her life."

Lucas laughed. "You wouldn't have thought so if you could have seen how she tried to keep me from seeing her cry all the way back to her apartment a little while ago." He sobered and stared at Ryan. "So you really do love her?"

"I do. I was on my way to talk to her and your family when I ran into you."

Lucas punched the button for the elevator and draped his arm over Ryan's shoulders. "Then let's go. She's back at her apartment. When I left, the whole family was gathered around her fussing over her. She probably needs rescuing by now."

The elevator doors opened, and they stepped inside. As they descended to the first floor, Ryan turned to Lucas. "Thanks for coming. I really appreciate it."

"No problem. If we're going to be brothers, you'd better get used to how I feel about my sister." He spread his index and middle fingers and wiggled them in Ryan's direction. "Just remember, I'll be watching you."

Then he laughed and clapped Ryan on the back.

Fifteen minutes later, they pulled to a stop at Jessica's apartment. Ryan pulled up behind Lucas and walked with him to the back door. He followed Lucas through the kitchen and hesitated at the doorway into the living room.

As Lucas entered, he heard Jessica's voice. "Lucas, where did you go? You left without saying a word."

"I had an errand to run. And I've brought someone with me. So if all of you except Jessica would be so kind as to step into the bedroom with me, I'd appreciate it."

"Lucas, what are you talking about?" she asked, exasperation in her voice.

Lucas stepped aside as Ryan entered the room. "Ryan needs to talk to Jessica," Lucas said as he strode toward what Ryan assumed was one of the bedrooms.

Ryan's gaze flitted over the other members of Jessica's family, noticing the surprised looks on their faces. After a moment, Adam took Claire by the hand and they hurried after Lucas. Jessica's parents hesitated only a moment longer before they, too, left the room.

Jessica rose from the sofa where she'd been sitting and stared at him, her eyes red from recent tears. He took a deep breath to rid himself of the tightness in his chest before he spoke. "I was on my way to see you when I ran into Lucas. He'd come to bring me back. He said you love me. Do you, Jessica?"

Her lips trembled, and then she frowned. "Do you want me to?"

He lunged forward until he stood in front of her. He reached up and gripped her shoulders. "More than I've ever wanted anything in my life. I've loved you ever since the first time I saw you at the precinct. At the time, I didn't want to involve you in all my problems, so I made the mistake of cutting you out of my life. I haven't had a peaceful day since. When I saw you at the convenience store, I nearly doubled over in shock. You were more beautiful than ever, and I wanted you more than I ever had."

"Then why didn't you tell me? Especially tonight after all we'd been through. I thought you'd only wanted me to help you with a case."

He shook his head. "No. I was afraid. Afraid that you hadn't forgiven me. Afraid your family wouldn't accept me. And most of all, afraid that you'd reject me and I'd be alone again."

She reached up and stroked his jaw. "I won't reject you. And neither will my family. I've been alone, too, Ryan, and I need you."

He pulled her so close that their breaths mingled as he moved his lips closer to hers. "I need you, too, Jessica. I love you."

"I love you, too," she whispered.

His lips crushed down on hers, and she strained upward to meet his kiss. After a moment, he released her mouth and trailed kisses down her cheek. "Marry me, Jessica. Please."

"Yes," she whispered. "I will."

He moved her away from him enough so that he could stare down into her eyes. "Do you mind living at my house or would you rather we get another one?"

Her eyes widened. "Of course I'll be happy there. Who wouldn't? It's a beautiful house, and I love the garden."

He smiled. "Do you really?"

"Of course I do."

He sighed. "I'm glad. Because I wasn't sure if I had made it just the way you described it or not."

Surprise flashed across her face. "What are you saying?"

"When Jamie and I moved in, the garden had been neglected, and I wanted to restore it. I remembered how you always talked about the backyard you wanted someday. As I began to work on it, I realized it was becoming exactly what you'd described, and I knew it was your garden. It was my way of keeping you in my life."

A tear trickled down the side of her cheek. "You made it for me? I can't believe it. And it's just what I always wanted." She looped her arms around his neck and smiled. "Oh, Ryan, I love you so much."

He gathered her close. "I love you, too. And you can do anything to the garden you want. Change anything. I only have one request for something I'd like to add to it."

"Anything," she said. "What is it?"

"A swing set with a big slide for our children to play on."

Her arms tightened around him. "That sounds perfect. I can hardly wait."

* * * * *

Dear Reader,

I hope you enjoyed reading the story of Ryan and Jessica's journey to reconciliation and a new commitment to each other. It is sad when a person lets misconceptions of another person's actions destroy relationships. Friendship and the love it provides are great treasures. We need to guard such relationships with great care. I Corinthians 13 is often called the Love Chapter and it speaks of charity, or love, and how God expects us to show it to our friends, our family and those we come in contact with each day. Among other things, we are called upon to bear all things, believe all things, hope all things and endure all things in love. When we do that, God will provide us the strength to get through the challenges of life. It is my prayer that we all will come to know that kind of love in our lives.

Sandra Robbins

COMING NEXT MONTH FROM
Love Inspired® Suspense

Available September 1, 2015

LISCNM0815

REQUEST YOUR FREE BOOKS!

2 FREE RIVETING INSPIRATIONAL NOVELS
PLUS 2 FREE MYSTERY GIFTS

Love Inspired.
SUSPENSE
RIVETING INSPIRATIONAL ROMANCE

YES! Please send me 2 FREE Love Inspired® Suspense novels and my 2 FREE mystery gifts (gifts are worth about $10). After receiving them, if I don't wish to receive any more books, I can return the shipping statement marked "cancel." If I don't cancel, I will receive 4 brand-new novels every month and be billed just $4.99 per book in the U.S. or $5.49 per book in Canada. That's a savings of at least 17% off the cover price. It's quite a bargain! Shipping and handling is just 50¢ per book in the U.S. and 75¢ per book in Canada.* I understand that accepting the 2 free books and gifts places me under no obligation to buy anything. I can always return a shipment and cancel at any time. Even if I never buy another book, the two free books and gifts are mine to keep forever.

123/323 IDN GH5Z

Name	(PLEASE PRINT)	
Address		Apt. #
City	State/Prov.	Zip/Postal Code

Signature (if under 18, a parent or guardian must sign)

Mail to the **Reader Service:**
IN U.S.A.: P.O. Box 1867, Buffalo, NY 14240-1867
IN CANADA: P.O. Box 609, Fort Erie, Ontario L2A 5X3

**Are you a current subscriber to Love Inspired® Suspense books
and want to receive the larger-print edition?
Call 1-800-873-8635 or visit www.ReaderService.com.**

* Terms and prices subject to change without notice. Prices do not include applicable taxes. Sales tax applicable in N.Y. Canadian residents will be charged applicable taxes. Offer not valid in Quebec. This offer is limited to one order per household. Not valid for current subscribers to Love Inspired Suspense books. All orders subject to credit approval. Credit or debit balances in a customer's account(s) may be offset by any other outstanding balance owed by or to the customer. Please allow 4 to 6 weeks for delivery. Offer available while quantities last.

Your Privacy—The Reader Service is committed to protecting your privacy. Our Privacy Policy is available online at www.ReaderService.com or upon request from the Reader Service.
We make a portion of our mailing list available to reputable third parties that offer products we believe may interest you. If you prefer that we not exchange your name with third parties, or if you wish to clarify or modify your communication preferences, please visit us at www.ReaderService.com/consumerchoice or write to us at Reader Service Preference Service, P.O. Box 9062, Buffalo, NY 14240-9062. Include your complete name and address.

LIS15

Lydia closed her eyes and tried to relax. But visions of the bombing assailed her mind. The sound of hideous laughter right before the bomb went off. The expression on Melinda's face when she knew what was going to happen. Was she alive? The feeling of helplessness she experienced trapped under the building debris. Her heartbeat began to race. A cold clamminess blanketed her.

Her hospital room door opened, pulling her away from the memories. When Lydia saw the person who entered, her pulse rate sped faster. Jesse Hunt. She wasn't prepared to see him.

He looked as if he'd come straight from the crime scene. As a search and rescue worker for Northern Frontier, he'd probably work as long as he could function. The only time he'd rest was when his K9 partner, Brutus, needed to.

So why is he here?

He stopped at the end of the bed. "Bree told me you were awake, so I took a chance and came to talk to you."

His stiff stance and white-knuckled hands on the railing betrayed his nervousness, but his tone told her he was here in his professional capacity. Saddened by that thought, Lydia said, "Thank you for finding me."

"I was doing my job yesterday."

"Knowing the people who would be searching kept my hope alive. Have you found everyone?"

"We don't know for sure. Names of missing people are still coming in. I was hoping you could tell me how many people were in the restaurant when the bomb exploded."

"I don't know…" The thought that the bistro was totally gone inundated her. She dropped her gaze to her lap, her hands quivering. Emotions crammed her throat. She turned for her water on the bedside table, but it was too far away. She started to lean forward and winced.

Jesse was at her side, grabbing the plastic cup and offering it to her.

She took it, and nearly splashed the water all over her with her shaking.

Jesse steadied the cup, then guided it to the bedside table. "I know this isn't easy, but anything you can remember could help us piece together what happened. We've got to stop this man."

"Nobody wants that more than me. I'm sure I'll remember more later." She hoped she could.

She needed to.

Don't miss
THE PROTECTOR'S MISSION
by Margaret Daley,
available September 2015 wherever
Love Inspired® Suspense books and ebooks are sold.

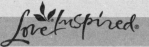

When a young Amish woman must choose between two very different brothers, will she find the husband of her heart?

Read on for a sneak preview of
THE AMISH BRIDE
The first book in the brand-new trilogy
LANCASTER COURTSHIPS

"I'm glad you came for ice cream, Ellen. I wanted to talk to you. Alone," Neziah said.

"*Dat!* Look at me!" Asa cried from the playground.

"I see you!" Neziah waved and looked back at Ellen. "Well, not *exactly* alone," he said wryly.

He continued. "I wanted to talk to you about this whole courting business. First, I want to apologize for my *vadder's*—" He shook his head. "I don't even know what to call it."

"You don't have to apologize, Neziah. My *vadder* was a part of it, too," she told him. "I know our parents mean well, but sometimes it might be better if they didn't get so…*involved*."

He smiled and looked down at his hands. "My father can sometimes be meddlesome, but this time I think our fathers might have a point."

Ellen looked at Neziah, thinking she must have misheard him. "You think…" She just stared at him for a moment in confusion. "You mean you think our fathers have a point in saying it's time we each thought about getting married?"

He met her gaze. He was the same Neziah she had once thought she was in love with, the same warm, dark eyes, but there was something different now. A confidence she hadn't recalled seeing on his plain face.

"Yes. And I think that you and I, Ellen—".he covered her hand with his "—should consider courting again."

Ellen was so shocked, it was a wonder she didn't fall off the picnic table bench. This was the last thing on earth she expected to hear from him. The warmth of his hand on hers made her shiver…and not unpleasantly. She pulled her hand away. "Neziah, I…"

"The past is the past," he said when she couldn't finish her thought. "We were both young then. But we're older now. Wiser. Neither of us is the same stubborn young person we once were." He kept looking at her, his gaze searching hers. "Ellen, I was in love with you once and I think—" he glanced at his boys "—I think I'm still in love with you." He looked back at her. "I *know* I am."

Don't miss
THE AMISH BRIDE by Emma Miller
available September 2015 wherever
Love Inspired® books and ebooks are sold.